HIDDEN HEROES

Published by Hellgate Press

(An imprint of L&R Publishing, LLC)

Hellgate Press

PO Box 3531

Ashland, OR 97520

email: info@hellgatepress.com

Interior & Cover Design: L. Redding

ISBN: 978-1-954163-26-3

Printed and bound in the United States of America

First edition 10 9 8 7 6 5 4 3 2 1

HIDDEN HEROES

AN AMERICAN REVOLUTIONARY WAR TALE

JAN FRAZIER

Hellgate Press   Ashland, Oregon

Dedicated to my late husband, Carl Frazier,
with whom I spent 37 wonderful years.
He was an awesome father, husband, and grandpa.

ACKNOWLEDGMENTS

I like to thank my best friend since first grade, Christy Wolfer Loy. With her expertise as an English teacher, she is always there for me when I need help in editing my books.

I'd also like to thank Karen Smith with whom I taught for many years, and she has been a faithful traveling companion on our many trips to Europe.

The Liberty Bell

TIMELINE OF THE REVOLUTIONARY WAR

March 22, 1765	The Stamp Act
March 5, 1770	Boston Massacre
Dec. 16, 1773	The Boston Tea Party
April 18, 1775	Paul Revere's ride
April 19, 1775	Lexington and Concord Battles: "The shot heard 'round the world"
May 10, 1775	Benedict Arnold, Ethan Arnold, and the Greene Mountain Boys seize Fort Ticonderoga
June 15, 1775	George Washington named Commander-in-Chief
June 17, 1775	Battle of Bunker Hill
Dec. 30, 1775	Benedict Arnold fails to seize Quebec
Jan. 15, 1776	Paine's Common Sense published
March 17, 1776	British evacuate Boston
July 4, 1776	Congress adopts Declaration of Independence
Aug 28, 1776	Redcoats defeat Washington's army in New York. Army escapes at night on Aug. 29
Sept. 21, 1776	Nathan Hale captured and hanged
Dec 26, 1776	Washington crosses the Delaware and captures Trenton
Jan 3, 1777	Washington victorious at Princeton
July 27, 1777	Lafayette arrives in Philadelphia
Fall, 1777	Washington makes plan for Culper spy ring
Sept. 11, 1777	British win at Brandywine, PA
Sept. 26, 1777	British occupy Philadelphia
Dec 19, 1777	Washington's army retires to Valley Forge
May 20, 1778	Battle of Barren Hill with Lafayette
June 18, 1778	British abandon Philadelphia and return to New York
June 28, 1778	Battle of Monmouth
June 20, 1779	Major General Lincoln inflicts major British casualties in South
Sept. 23, 1780	John Andre arrested, leading to the exposure of Benedict Arnold's plan to cede West Point to the British.
Oct 14, 1780	Washington names Nathanael Greene commander of South
Jan. 17, 1781	American General Daniel Morgan defeats Colonel

	Tarleton at Cowpens, SC
April 25, 1781	Greene defeated and leaves for home
Oct. 19, 1781	Cornwallis surrounded on land and sea; surrenders at Yorktown, VA
Sept. 3, 1783	USA and Great Britain sign Treaty of Paris
Nov. 25, 1783	British troops leave New York City
Nov. 25, 1783	Washington bids goodbye to his troops
Dec. 23, 1783	Washington resigns as Commander

INTRODUCTION

A merica was born of a revolution. It began with a single shot fired in a small New England village – Lexington. For nine generations, the people of this vast frontier had considered themselves loyal British-Americans; however, they considered themselves foremost Virginians, New Yorkers, and Pennsylvanians. Residents of thirteen colonies stretched along the eastern edge of an untamed land.

New taxes and forbiddance of settling the western frontier caused the New Englanders to resist the British, rebel, and finally revolt. April 18, 1775, was the eve of the greatest insurrection America had ever seen.

Nathan Hoyt is fifth generation grandparent from me and was born in Norwalk, Connecticut, on April 28, 1719. He married Elizabeth Lockwood, who bore him eleven children. He fought in the American Revolution, but I have no knowledge of his exact position in the army. He was not among the Culper Spy Ring, but for fictional interest, I made him a member.

Nathan Hoyt, Jr., (renamed Job for the book) was one of Nathan Hoyt's eleven children, and he also served in the Revolutionary War.

John Champe, born in 1751, is fourth generation grandparent from my friend, Christy Wolfer Loy and was an actual member of the Culper Spy Ring. General George Washington himself declared that Champe's undertaking to kidnap Benedict Arnold was the most dangerous, secret mission of the Revolutionary

War. Champe was given this assignment because Washington was said to have the greatest confidence in Champe.

The battles and most of the numerous stories in the novel are all true and accurate, to the best of my ability.

To be clear with the terms used in the book: The English were called Redcoats, Regulars, Lobsters, Tories, and Loyalists. Americans were called Minutemen, Continental Army, Patriots, Sons of Liberty, and Rebels.

The Americans – when the war first began – still thought of themselves as British. Thus, Paul Revere never said, "The British are coming." In reality, he said, "The Regulars are coming."

Beginning with Chapter 4, all of the evenly numbered chapters are telling the reader what is happening back at the Hoyt household in Lexington. The unevenly numbered chapters are about the battles and what is happening in Nathan Hoyt's world as a soldier and spy.

Washington's Spy Ring was as follows (Code names are shown in parentheses):

~ Robert Townsend (Samuel Culper, Jr., 723) reported to Abraham Woodhull (Samuel Culper, Sr, 722)

~ Anna Strong (355) reported Caleb Brewster's whereabouts to Abraham Woodhull (Samuel Culper, Sr., 722)

~ Abraham Woodhull reported to Caleb Brewster (725)

~ Caleb Brewster gave message to Austin Roe (724)

~ Austin Roe reported to Benjamin Tallmadge (John Bolton 721)

~ Benjamin Tallmadge gave message to Nathan Hoyt (726)

~ Nathan Hoyt reported to General Washington (711)

~ John Champe attempted to kidnap Benedict Arnold but failed.

In case the reader gets confused with the commanders (if they are British or American), all of the commanders are Americans, except for the following who are British: John Pitcairn, Johann Rall, Banastre Tarleton, Henry Clinton, John Simcoe, Charles Cornwallis, Thomas Gage, and John Andre (spy for the British), and eventually Benedict Arnold (became a traitor to America).

The Old North Church, Boston, MA

CHAPTER 1

THE REGULARS ARE COMING!

Nathan Hoyt sat on a porch swing on the cold, damp April night. Although it should have been only dusk, darkness had swallowed the day along with the stars and moon. A light drizzle dripped from the somber sky. Two dogs yelped in the distance, disturbing the otherwise hushed silence of April 18, 1775. What Nathan didn't know at this serene and subdued moment in Lexington was that peace and tranquility was about to end for the continent of colonies.

After 10:00 p.m., two lanterns glowed briefly in Boston's Old North Church tower – just long enough to signal the New Englanders that Redcoats would move that night by water toward Concord. Although the cobblestone streets and the leaden roofs were wet, the light rain had ceased in Boston, and a slice of golden moon was rising in the east as forty-year-old Paul Revere mounted his horse to begin his famous fifteen-mile ride to Lexington and on to Concord.

Nathan Hoyt, father of eleven children, had earlier watched his wife, Elizabeth, lay a mat on the floor in front of the fire so the children could play checkers. Only four children still remained at home while the other seven were grown and lived nearby.

Elizabeth busied herself with household duties in the kitchen. There was much to do yet before she could contemplate sitting by the fire and knitting.

Nathan sat on the porch attempting to understand the turmoil he was feeling inside – or was it outside? He couldn't put his finger on it, but it was as palpable and as tangible as the gust of icy wind that had just hit his face.

Unexpectedly, Elizabeth opened the door leading to the porch.

"Nathan, I made tea. Would you like some?"

He nodded without verbally answering.

"What's wrong, Nathan? Why are you out here? You'll catch a chill."

Elizabeth was still attractive even in her forties. Her dark blonde hair was streaked with a little gray, but she possessed a smile that was engaging and often playful, despite the difficult life in the colonies.

"I'll get the tea. Why don't you come inside?"

Nathan got up from the swing, still staring into the ebony night sky, wishing to see the steeples of the nearby church as they climbed into the heavens. He entered the house, which was a moderately large structure that had once housed all eleven children plus Nathan's father, Daniel, who years before had died of a stroke.

Nathan was tall and well built like his father. Inheriting a large section of land when his father passed, Nathan and his grown son and sons-in-law now farmed forty acres of land adjacent to their house.

"Sit by the fire, Nathan, and I will get us both a mug of tea. Is something bothering you? You have not said a word," Elizabeth remarked, gazing intently at her husband.

Nathan shunned Elizabeth's question and inconspicuously nodded toward the children.

"Later," he whispered, and she understood.

"Pa, come help me," begged Gracie, who was getting beat by her brother Nate. "I think Nate is cheating. You know, moving checkers when I am not looking. Would you take my place and try to beat him?"

Nathan was really too tired from the long day, but checkers was a diversion that he needed. He slid over to the mat as Grace moved to give him room. Elizabeth brought his tea, and Nathan settled in. Samuel – nearly a man at age fourteen – rose to get another log for the fire.

The checker games went on for an hour when Elizabeth declared it was bedtime.

"You children have early chores and then school tomorrow. Get into your night clothes, and Pa and I will be in to say prayers."

The two girls slept in one room and the two boys in the other. It was quite a change from having four children per room when all eleven were at home. Elizabeth took the girls' room as Nathan sat with the boys to say nightly prayers.

"Lord, thank you for being with us today as we started our early plowing. Give us strength as the spring blossoms, and provide us with rain for our crops once they are planted." Nathan paused, obviously weighing his next sentence. "And, Lord, give us peace now and in the future days. Amen."

There was a moment of silence as the boys focused on their father. Finally, Samuel questioned, "Why are you asking for peace? Do you know something we don't, Pa?"

Nathan lifted his gaze, peering at his sons.

"No, not really, son. It was simply an idle comment, meaning nothing."

To take the edge off, Nathan jostled Nate's hair as he said goodnight to them both.

Nathan ambled into his bedroom to don his bedclothes. Elizabeth was sitting on the bed, apparently waiting for her husband.

She remained silent for only a moment before she asked, "Nathan, what is wrong? Is it something with the children?"

Nathan shook his head. Finally, he glanced intently at his wife and cleared his throat. "Have you ever 'felt' something in the air, Elizabeth?"

Elizabeth sat, thinking for a bit.

"Actually, yes, I have. The first time we met, I physically felt love all around me," Elizabeth replied with a grin. Nathan returned the smile.

"However," Elizabeth continued, "I also often feel God around me, giving me advice that seems confusing during difficult, trying times."

"Well, I can only say that I was not feeling love tonight out there on the porch, and I would relish having some advice from the Lord. No, what I'm feeling is neither of those but rather a sense of uneasiness – apprehension," divulged Nathan. "There's something palpable out there – something so intense that it is almost tangible."

"Well, dear, you have had a hard day in starting to clear the fields. The first few days are always particularly tiring. However, to add to all of that, you even had to clean and oil some of the farm equipment that you couldn't attend to last fall with that early blizzard we had in late October," continued. Elizabeth. "We were lucky just to get to the barn to feed the animals. I said all of that just to say you had a particularly difficult and busy day today."

"Yes, that's true. However, it is not the work that's bothering me. I just really cannot put my finger on it, Elizabeth."

Elizabeth returned to the kitchen to finish the last of the dishes, and when she returned, she found Nathan on his knees praying – something Nathan seldom did except when he was troubled. The two often prayed together in bed but getting onto his knees meant that he was seriously worried about something.

"What time is it, Elizabeth?" Nathan asked as she knelt down, too, to put her arms around her husband.

"Nearing eleven o'clock. You had better get to sleep, love. It'll be another long day tomorrow. There's never a let-up once you start in the fields."

Nathan nodded. He crawled into bed, but sleep didn't come. He lay there staring at the ceiling, still feeling the tension that had overcome him on the porch. He was restless – an edgy feeling still consumed him – and he quietly got up to walk to the living area to sit by the fire. Gazing at the soft glow of smoldering logs often took his mind off dilemmas. Tonight, though, they just looked like logs simmering down to a slow burn, and it gave him no rest.

Nathan sat in a chair with his hands clasped, and at first, he thought that he was imagining a far-off noise. He listened carefully and soon realized that the sound was real. Nathan quickly got up and went to the door.

Flinging it open, Nathan stepped onto the porch. He listened again. There it was once more! No way that it was imagined. It was loud and clear.

"The Regulars are coming. The Regulars are coming."

Old North Bridge, Concord, MA

CHAPTER 2

THE SHOT HEARD 'ROUND THE WORLD

Paul Revere had left the old North Church in Boston – astride Brown Beauty, the fastest horse he could find – where lanterns indicated the route of the British: "One if by land; two if by sea." On April 18, the two lanterns signaled the river route of British troops, who were heading to Concord. Were the Redcoats also after the Continental leaders housed in Lexington?

Yes, the British were after both John Hancock and Samuel Adams, two of the principal troublemakers of uprisings in the colonies plus leaders in the Congress. They were staying with Reverend Jonas Clark, and Revere was attempting to warn them. However, General Thomas Gage had twin objectives to his plan. Not only was he after Hancock and Adams, but he also was to proceed to Concord and destroy an arsenal that contained stocks of rebel weaponry and powder.

Nathan Hoyt quickly dressed, grabbed his musket, and kissed Elizabeth. His four young children were still asleep in bed as Nathan scrambled to join his friends and neighbors at Buckman's Tavern. Revere had passed the tavern fifteen minutes earlier, and Nathan now found it restlessly astir with rumors, lights, and men.

Meanwhile, Dr. Samuel Prescott had been courting his sweet-heart when the hour grew late. As Dr. Prescott – well known for being one of the "Sons of Liberty" – rode home, he was joined by two Concord-bound riders: Paul Revere and his friend William Dawes.

Officers seemed to be waiting for Revere, and he later told the story: "In an instant, I saw four officers who rode up to me with their pistols in their hands and told me to stop. If I were to go an inch further, I'd be shot."

In the end, Revere was taken prisoner, and Dawes escaped on foot through the woods. However, Dr. Prescott, who knew the land even in the dark, jumped his horse over a stone wall and reached Concord, heralding the news of the Redcoats coming.

Seeing his son Job appear in the doorway of the tavern, Nathan went to stand with him. At age twenty-two, Job was an image of his father. Being the only son of Nathan who was old enough to fight, Job stood tall and straight with his musket at his side. Married to Anna Raymond for three years, they had a two-year-old son and a newborn daughter. Most of the 130 men – called Minutemen because of their speed to act – had families whom they all wished to protect.

The Minutemen – mostly dairy farmers and a few craftsmen – passed the chilly hours before daybreak beside the hearth of Buckman's Tavern. As the night wore on and the drizzle dissipated, the sun peeked its head over the eastern horizon. It was April 19, 1775 – a day that would go down in history. As it grew light, Captain John Parker assembled his Minutemen into two lines with the drummer boy sounding the beat. They stood on the road that led to Concord, awaiting the Redcoats, who were coming from Boston.

Captain Parker's immortal command to his men was ordered in courage. "Stand your ground, men; don't fire unless fired upon; but if the Regulars mean to have war, let it begin here" in Lexington.

The Minutemen heard the Redcoats long before they saw them as the drummer beat out the rhythmic percussion. General Gage's original plan was to set his troops in motion before midnight, complete the operation in Concord by 8:00, and have his militia safely back in Boston by noon, well before the Minutemen could respond. Obviously, it didn't happen that way.

As the Redcoats finally entered the green, they moved head-on toward the Minutemen. Another British commander in charge of the army, Major John Pitcairn, was astride his horse and yelled to the Continental Army, "Disperse, ye Rebels! Lay down your arms!"

Before that could happen, a shot rang out – from where and from whom, no one knew – but it echoed through history as "the shot heard around the world." Similar to a brain concussion that erases the memory of the blow that caused it, that first shot echoed unidentified throughout history. In that single puff of smoke, the bond between the English and the Americans was severed.

As the day wore on, the fighting intensified, and the carnage continued on the battlefield, which extended 200 yards wide and sixteen miles long. The Continental Army was enraged as shock of the battle finally registered in their minds, and, in the end, an east wind cleared the smoke, leaving eight Americans dead with nine wounded. A few of the Americans who were shot down and lay injured were then bayoneted to death by the English, who were now caught up in a frenzy of passion for the war. By 9:00 on that soft spring day, the Redcoats had won their victory and continued on to Concord as the colonists retreated.

Nathan went home long enough to tell Elizabeth that he was going on to Concord.

"While I'm gone, melt down some of the pewter pots so that I have more ammunition. I'm afraid that this is just the start of battles to come," stated Nathan.

"Oh, please, be careful, Nathan. Don't take unnecessary chances," pleaded Elizabeth.

"Pa, can I come along?" chimed in fourteen-year-old Samuel.

"No, son, you must stay here and help your mother. While I'm away, you know that you must be the man of the house."

Samuel sadly nodded.

All the Lexington Minutemen shouldered their rifles, setting off toward Concord to vent their grief in Redcoat blood. The militia grew steadily during the next few hours, and by early afternoon, more than a thousand soldiers were present, giving the Americans superiority in numbers for the first time that day. Plus, by the time they reached Concord, the Americans were no longer reluctant to kill the king's soldiers.

As the afternoon sun slowly began to set, the Redcoats relinquished the battle at Concord to return to Boston. They had 270 soldiers either wounded, missing, or dead. In addition, the Redcoats had found little ammunition in the supply depots that they had gone to destroy. In reality, most of Concord's munitions had been transferred elsewhere following an alert from Boston's leaders two weeks earlier that the British were coming to decimate the artillery. The small amount of ammunition that the British did find they punctured or threw into the nearby river.

That night, every leader, soldier, and civilian who had witnessed the battles knew that the day's events had changed their world forever.

* * * *

Well past dusk, Nathan returned home, exhausted but satisfied that they had given the Redcoats a taste of their own medicine.

With the children still awake, Nathan didn't want to tell of the horrors he had seen. Instead, he decided to educate the family – Hannah, Samuel, Grace, and Nate – on the music that the Redcoats sang as they marched to Concord.

"The fifes and drums were playing, and the soldiers were singing 'Yankee Doodle' as they made their way to Concord. The Redcoats wanted to make sure that we all heard the song in its entirety."

"What does it mean?" asked Gracie. "'Yankee Oodle?'"

Elizabeth and Nathan exchanged glances and smiles.

"Well, the entire song is an insult to us colonists," answered Nathan. "'Yankee Doodle' refers to all of us as country bumpkins – useless country folks who have no idea how to fight."

Nathan stopped to ponder a moment. "I think that whatever honors we achieved today we can add the fact that we Yankee Doodles know how to fight. Do you know that, in the end, there were a thousand Americans who turned out today from towns within a fifty-mile radius to fight the British? We've not been trained as soldiers, but we knew how to use the rifle, and we showed the Redcoats that we weren't afraid of them."

To be fair, the colonists were not yet an official army at all. They had no flag, no uniforms, and no official training. They had been referred to at first as the Continental Army by the colonists and as Rebels by the British. It wasn't long, though, before they became "the American army." It was an army of men accustomed to hard work as farmers, shoemakers, carpenters, blacksmiths, ship builders, sailors, and fishermen. Most knew from experience the hardships and setbacks of a difficult life. Thus, preparing for the worst was second nature to most of the soldiers.

Nevertheless, to be sure, some of the men had no trade at

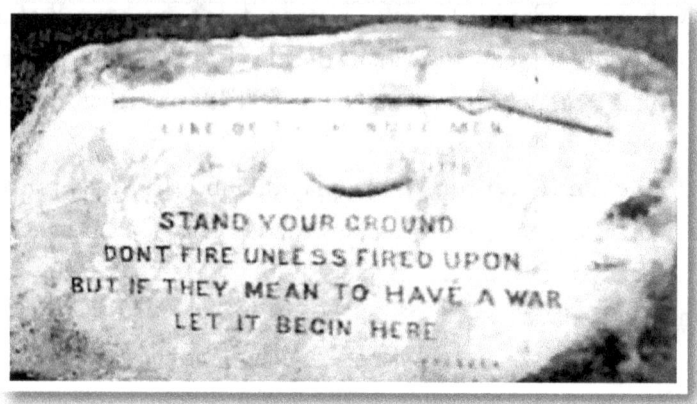

Commerative stone in Lexington, MA

all. They were drifters, tavern lowlife, or riffraff of society. However, by and large, most were good, solid citizens who were married, with their families depending on them. It was, indeed, the first American army, all composed of men of different colors. There were countless nationalities – America was already a melting pot – and there were various degrees of education and physical conditions. Some were not even men but rather smooth-faced boys of sixteen years of age.

In contrast to the Continental army, the official Redcoats were actually full-time soldiers only because they didn't fit into the English society proper. Many were the dregs of society and had failed as farmers, weavers, or shop owners. Many were, in fact, ex-convicts. They had nowhere to go except to the military where they were trained to fight.

Although trained for European fighting, they were not accustomed to working the harsh environment and land of New England with rugged hills, rocks, and brush throughout the landscape. In addition, the Redcoats had little self-discipline. Gambling, pandering, arguing over local women, and drinking heavily were very common among the British soldiers.

All in all, the colonists were willing to learn the ways of an American army. Indeed, no one knew what was in store for him as there had been no colonial army previously. If he had known the hardships, tears, blood, and fears, would he have continued on with this newly formed group who would soon be known as the Patriots? Nathan Hoyt and his son, Job, along with every other man who fought in Lexington and Concord that day – April 19, 1775 – would have a one-word answer – YES!

The Boston Tea Party, 1763

CHAPTER 3

LEAVING HOME

For the next week, conversations at Buckman's Tavern were centered around the Redcoats. It was obvious to everyone that this was the start of a war, but the colonists all thought that it would be over by winter.

"This war will be short lived. We'll be celebrating Christmas as a free country with our families," was the consensus of opinion.

It was true that life had become a pandemonium to the colonists. One day they had been at peace, living their day-to-day lives, and the next day they were fighting an actual war – a war not in Europe but right in the colonies.

It was at this point that Nathan and Job were deciding what they should do. Should they fight with the Minutemen? Should they follow the militia to any given battle? Should they stay in Lexington and fight only if the Redcoats returned?

"Pa, you're a natural leader. Why don't you go to Philadelphia and see if army captains are training people to help lead?" suggested Job.

"I don't know, son. I'm kind of a back woodsman since I was brought up to hunt and to farm."

"But your hunting skills are perfect," remarked Job.

"For animals maybe but not enemies – soldiers, no less, who have had expert training."

"But, Pa, your years spent with your Oneida friends taught you everything you need to know to fight the enemy."

Nathan thought for a moment about what his son had said. He did have all the hiding and shooting techniques as taught to him by his friend, Little Bear, of the Oneidas. Certainly, the Redcoats had only marching skills and then the non-skills of standing in full view and shooting. Was this really expert training?

Not responding immediately to his son, Nathan decided to ponder the thought. He knew that for him it was a must to join the militia one way or another. What could be lost by going to Philadelphia and seeing if he were qualified to teach soldiers to hunt with his tactics? Or, perhaps, he would be trained to fight in a different way – a new American way.

Finally, Nathan Hoyt decided to leave Lexington and move towards Philadelphia. If he found an army that needed help between Lexington and Philadelphia, so be it. He'd attach himself to it. Job, in the end, decided to join his father. They were, after all, a good team.

"I think that we should stay another few months in Lexington to plant all of the crops and then leave it up to the children at home, your older sisters and their husbands to be responsible for the duties of the farm," Nathan said to Job. "I don't enjoy making this decision; however, our country needs us … at least me."

"Yes, me, too, Pa. I'm just glad that my brothers-in-law will be here to assist."

"Well, that's possibly temporary because I think that the military will soon tell all young men that they have to enlist, probably for a year. Then they will have a chance at the end of the year to reenlist," commented Nathan.

By early 1776, all eligible men would be sequestered to join the colonists in the battle against the British. By the fall, with some reluctance, all six husbands had to leave the Hoyt sisters and their children and take up arms in various platoons.

* * * *

During Nathan's last weeks at home, evening supper conversations were concentrated on the newly acquired war with the British. Each night the children were asking about something else that was discussed at school.

"Why can't we just move West and get away from all of this fighting?" asked Samuel one night.

"Well, you may have been too young to remember, Samuel, but your mother and I deliberated on settling on the Western Frontier, but the British forbid us from doing that," commented Nathan.

"What? Why?" continued Samuel.

"England has very limited lands onto which citizens can settle. If the English allow the Americans to settle further west here, then they will have everyone leaving England for the New World," concluded Nathan.

"However," Elizabeth inserted, "that's not to say that we won't move in the future."

"Pa, our teacher mentioned the Stamp Act today, but it wasn't explained. What exactly was that?" asked Samuel.

"Well, son, in 1765, England was heavily in debt so they passed the Stamp Act to raise funds. You see, we colonists came to believe that anytime the British needed money, something was done to us to help reduce their debt." Nathan paused a moment to think of how to explain the Stamp Act so that it would be understood by the children.

"The Stamp Act required that the British government-issued stamps be placed on all legal documents and newspapers. All of this paper was produced in London with an embossed revenue stamp and then sent to America for purchase. Therefore, if any item had a stamp, then we had to pay an extra tax. Our mother country managed to anger not only local political leaders, but also many members of our colonial society, who then took their protests to the streets. In fact, Paul Revere – who warned us that night of April 18 about the Regulars coming – led many demonstrations against the British, especially against the Stamp Act. In addition, you may remember, Samuel, Job and I joined in the political action in Lexington that one summer and marched to Boston to protest the Stamp Act."

"Now that you mention it, I do, but I was too young to actually understand what was happening," proclaimed Samuel.

Elizabeth picked up where Nathan had left off. "We colonists grew tired of being unfairly taxed and, well, bullied by the British. People became enraged and refused to buy British goods, and many of our friends who owned their own shops in Lexington had to make the decision of saying 'no' to selling British goods."

"Didn't you quit buying sugar? I remember that because there were no cookies baked for a while," Samuel piped in.

"Yes, there was a boycott put on all kinds of things," continued Elizabeth, "such as gloves, hats, clothing, sugar, flour, and many other things. It was a boycott of anything coming from England because we were so mad about The Stamp Act."

"Ma, what does boycott mean?" questioned Hannah.

Elizabeth turned to Hannah. "It means that no one will buy it, or you avoid it."

Hannah asked with a sly grin, "Oh, like I could boycott school?"

"You would never do that, darling, because you are such a good student," responded Elizabeth, returning her daughter's grin.

"Speaking of Paul Revere," chimed in Grace, "our teacher told us that Revere – who is a silversmith by trade – founded the first patriot intelligence network in Boston. The group was known as the 'Mechanics.' I didn't know any of this, and I've always been fascinated about spy rings. My teacher also told us that he was a member of the Sons of Liberty, who demonstrated not only against the Stamp Act but also against many of the British laws."

"Yes," responded Nathan, "I have heard of the 'Mechanics.' Apparently, they spied on British soldiers and formed their plans regularly at the Green Dragon Tavern in Boston. I only recently heard these details, Grace."

"Sorry to change the subject, but I have a question now," inserted Nate. "The class was talking about the Boston Massacre the other day. Explain that to me."

Elizabeth nodded to Nathan to respond. "Well, actually we colonists sort of started that. It occurred on March 5, 1770, and we were mad about how we had been treated with taxes, and there was a group of Americans in the Boston harbor. The British were on ships, and we were yelling 'you scoundrels and Lobsters.' It didn't incite them enough and so we then started throwing rocks at them. That did it, and someone on the ship yelled 'fire,' and five Americans fell."

"Only five fell?" questioned Samuel. "A massacre sounds as if lots of people were killed."

"Well, I believe that it had to do with the fact that the British soldiers were firing on an innocent crowd who had no weapons, and, again, it made us question our future with the British empire. They didn't treat us well sometimes," concluded Nathan.

"And why did the colonists call the British 'Lobsters'?" said Nate.

Nathan smiled. "It was short for 'Lobsterbacks' or 'Bloody-backs.' Because of their long red coats, they resembled lobsters. And, of course, because the coats were red, that reminded the colonists of blood. We did this to taunt them, and it really wasn't nice of us. Your ma and I always try to teach you to be sweet to people even if you don't like them, and yet the colonists were not always nice."

There was silence for a bit as the children finished up their meal and awaited the pudding that Elizabeth had made.

"Pa," Gracie chimed in, "tell us about the Boston Tea Party. You have told us before, but it's interesting and kind of unbelievable."

"Well, the Tea Act of 1773 allowed the British to drive out foreign teas and assured the East India Company a monopoly on the drink. That meant that we could only buy East Indian tea. Well, we assumed that once the monopoly was in place, then the British government would raise prices, and we would be stuck. If the British could tax tea, then they could possibly tax all British goods."

"Like you said, Pa, the British haven't always been good to us, huh?" inquired Gracie.

"Often that has been so, Gracie. Well, the Americans were mad, and on December 16, 1773, under the cover of darkness, some of the colonists posed as Mohawk Native Americans and climbed onto the ship which housed the tea. They dumped the 342 chests of tea into the Boston harbor.

"Because of incidents like the Tea Party, it was in September 1774 that our first Continental Congress was held, and the members issued a third boycott on all British-made goods. Looking back on history, one could say that a war *per se* has been an ongoing battle for ten years," concluded Nathan. "It looked as though it started on April 19, but in reality, it started years ago."

* * * *

Nathan and Job stayed home longer than they had anticipated. It was not until fall that the two were ready to depart. As
can be imagined, saying goodbye to the family was a difficult
task for the two men. Many questions remained. Would Nathan
and Job see them again? Would this be goodbye forever? Would
they return but minus an arm or leg?

Their friend George Kahill had recently returned from the
Battle of Bunker Hill without an arm. It was impossible to keep
any of the colonists down, and George was no different. He
was no stranger to a difficult life, and now, unable to farm with
only one arm, George sold the farmland and opened a tavern
between Lexington and Concord.

George told them the story of Bunker Hill. Nathan and Job
had both heard it before, but they wanted to learn what George
had to say about it.

"On the night of June 16, some 1,200 Americans moved to
Bunker Hill – well, really it was Breed's Hill because we got
confused in the dark – and we had picks and shovels to build a
fortification," stated George. "We were not quiet during the
night. It was impossible to be with the picks and shovels hitting
the earth. The British knew that we were doing something but
had no idea what. I'm sure that the Redcoats were astonished
in the morning to see that we had built the redoubt so well.
After all, we were just Yankee Doodles." George smiled at his
sarcasm.

Nathan and Job also smiled. "What did the redoubt look
like?" asked Job.

"Well, it was four-sided – a square fortification. Each side
was said to be about 140 feet, and the walls were tall and steep.

We had done a good job despite the darkened conditions," asserted George.

"What happened then?" questioned Nathan.

"Well, we fought incessantly. One of my friends, Israel Putnam, shouted to all who could hear, 'Fire low. Every one of you can kill a squirrel at a hundred yards. Pick off the commanders.'

"We drove the Redcoats back a couple of times during the day of June 17. You know, during this fight, I discovered the terror that exists in the last seconds prior to combat. Many of us had never been in any kind of battle, and it is a gut-wrenching moment until that shot is taken – one that seems to last an eternity."

George didn't talk much of the real carnage that he had witnessed, but he did mention that one of his friends died.

"Jacob was a long-time friend of mine and was shot in several places. He was in a bad way with no medical supplies available. He ended up bleeding to death," remarked George, his eyes downcast.

"How did you survive?" questioned Nathan.

"I was lucky because I had a few supplies in my knapsack, and a friend tightly bound up my arm with a tourniquet. It saved my life, but not my arm."

George insisted over and over that the greatest casualty at Bunker Hill was the British myth of Yankee cowardice. "I know the Redcoats won the battle, but they were shocked at our enthusiasm and rage that fell upon them. After all, while the British were fighting for the King and money, we Americans were fighting for our freedom."

And it was just this thirst for freedom that the Hoyt men carried with them.

* * * *

Meanwhile, the first Continental Congress of Philadelphia

chose Colonel George Washington to lead the war. Assuring his wife, Martha, that he would be home by Christmas, Washington left for Boston. He would be home for Christmas – just eight years later than expected.

Washington had attained a fairly quick ascent in his limited military career during his younger years and then won Ohio for Great Britain in 1758. In addition, it was at this time that Washington took a step that attributed to his fast advancement in the colonies – he not only married Martha Custis, but he also inherited Mount Vernon from his brother who had recently died.

In the 1760s Washington began to take an active role in the Virginia protest movement against British's new colonial policies, and he was named one of the seven delegates to the Continental Congress.

Now at age forty-three, Washington remained an imposing figure. With the average American being about 5-foot, 8-inches tall, 150 pounds, George Washington towered over them with his 6-foot, 3-inch stature and weight of 225 pounds. With his new position, Colonel Washington became General George Washington.

Sometime after Washington was elected to lead the Continental Army, Thomas Paine came from England and settled in America. It seemed as if during these early days of fighting the British, no one had declared if Americans were fighting for true independence from England or just reconciliation with England. Thomas Paine had a taste for assertion and possessed a refreshing talent for writing. His electrifying document captured what most Americans – as well as most congressmen – were feeling.

In his forty-seven-page document entitled *Common Sense*, Paine proposed destroying the monarchy under which Americans lived and establishing a new government. It was a folly to believe in a hereditary monarch, and it was no less gloomy to believe in reconciliation. "Ye that dare oppose not only the tyranny but the tyrants, stand forth!" Paine promoted the question of independence to the top of the political agenda.

No one expected that half-a-million copies of *Common Sense* would be sold to the colonists. America had turned a corner. The sentiment for independence increased in the following weeks as word from England declared that King George III was thinking of gathering German mercenaries to suppress the American rebellion. If the King took that step, then America would "declare the colonies in a state of Independent Sovereignty."

For the first time, Thomas Paine's document was saying exactly what the Americans were thinking – they wanted independence from Britain!

* * * *

During the winter of 1775, everyone's eyes were on Boston. With the Redcoat army housed there, it was apparent that they held the city without any problem, and, by now, the colonists were attempting to fight them with very little artillery in their possession. What the colonists needed were cannons.

Earlier in the year, Captain Benedict Arnold had foreseen this need. He had often passed Fort Ticonderoga on his way to Quebec when he had been trading horses. The Fort had been a rotting relic from the French and Native American War, but it had housed a large storehouse of artillery. In addition, if the colonists could have seized the Fort, they could have blocked the British on the road coming down from Canada.

That spring, Ethan Allen had teamed up with Benedict Arnold and the Green Mountain Boys and had moved toward the

British-held Fort Ticonderoga, in an effort to apprehend the large storehouse of artillery and cannons. Before dawn in May 1775, the soldiers had stormed the gates, surprising the sleeping British soldiers and had demanded the surrender of the forty-five-man garrison. In ten bloodless minutes, the Americans had taken Fort Ticonderoga and its cannons, now much needed in Boston.

That winter, General Henry Knox went to Fort Ticonderoga and retrieved the artillery that Washington needed in Boston. General Washington had set it up in Dorchester Heights near Boston. British General William Howe, who was stationed in Boston with the Redcoats, awoke one morning to find Dorchester Heights beset with rows of cannons and artillery. Fearing for their lives, Howe and his men retreated from Boston. What Howe didn't know was that Washington had a great number of weapons but had no ammunition. It was all a bluff. Washington had won his first victory without fighting a battle.

About that same time, Benedict Arnold developed a grandiose plan to invade Canada and establish a victory over the British in that country. Arnold, who was relying on bad maps, guessed the distance at 180 miles – a journey of less than three weeks. In reality, the army traveled 250 miles in forty-six days, and the route through the wilderness was nothing short of gruesome. The project was full of danger – an uncarefully mapped frontier, Native Americans of doubtful alliance, tempers of the Canadians, and the threat of bad weather.

In spite of all adversities, Arnold's army made its way toward Quebec. In his platoon, even two soldiers' wives shared and survived the hardships of the desperate route, winning the respect of all. However, with bloody battles, smallpox outbreaks, and icy cold weather with little food, the Americans finally had to relent and retreat home. These brave warriors must have wondered if they would ever know the comforts of home again. Even Nathan Hoyt pondered that thought as he wrote home to his beloved wife, Elizabeth.

CHAPTER 4

LETTER FROM NATHAN AND AT HOME IN LEXINGTON

Dearest Elizabeth,

It has been a long, slow journey toward Philadelphia, and we're not close yet. Job and I have stopped often to help people in need of manpower, fight in small battles, and attend to wounded soldiers.

We've stopped nearly daily at farmhouses to ask for food. Sometimes if it were at mealtime, we were invited in to sit and eat with the family. Other times, we were given bread, cheese, and dried meat to eat along the way. Everyone has been very accommodating.

Recently, Job and I had the privilege of meeting General Henry Knox while we were at a militia site in Massachusetts. He was in charge of a platoon, and he actually sat one night while we were there and talked with us. If you remember, he brought the artillery from Fort Ticonderoga to Boston.

Knox is a very imposing man, stout and more than six feet tall. He dwarfed most of the men in his platoon. In addition, he's very young. I had no idea. I think that he's about 25. He is jokingly called Little Ox because he used 80 yokes of oxen to bring the artillery from Fort Ticonderoga to Boston. It must have been quite a trip.

He told us as we all sat around the fire that night that he was the son of an English immigrant, and that he had dropped out of school and gone to work for a bookseller at age thirteen. Knox said that now when he is not leading the military, he is reading whatever he can get his hands on. I guess that I haven't thought of our military leaders as being interested in literature. We often forget that they are normal people with a "real" life outside of the military.

All of us soldiers loved getting to chat with Knox and learn about him. Amazingly, he talked openly about himself; most generals don't do that.

That same night, Job and I met Patrick—I never knew his last name—who told us that he had been robbed the previous week by some strangers who had been in the platoon for a day.

Patrick had taken off his coat and waistcoat because it had been warm, and his pocketbook containing five dollars had been in his waistcoat. The strangers were very chatty, asking many questions. Without being asked, they helped with the fire to cook and just seemed very friendly and nice.

However, Patrick said, that he soon learned that those kind-hearted helpers had availed themselves of the opportunity to snag his pocketbook. By the time that he discovered this, they were long gone from the platoon. He cautioned us to be aware of strangers. I'm so glad that he told us this because both Job and I are so trust-

ing of people—friends as well as strangers. It had, at least, put us on the lookout to be wary.

Job and I left that group of soldiers the next day and walked all morning and afternoon until we finally saw a large farmhouse. We hadn't been able to find clean water anywhere in the streams. All we could find were nasty frog ponds, thick with mud and filth. The farm had a well with good, clean water so we drank copiously.

In addition, by the time we found the farmhouse, it was past dusk, and we were hoping for a place to spend the night. We asked if we could sleep the night on the floor near the fire. The lady-of-the-house put down mats in the living area for us near the fire, and we had a snug place to sleep.

The lady had a spaniel similar to Beauty, and she snuggled right in with us. It felt like home! The kind lady fixed us a warm breakfast in the morning that was totally unexpected but certainly appreciated.

I send my love to you and the children and pray that you are safe and well.

Your devoted husband,
Nathan

* * * *

Although Nathan had been gone just ten months, the time seemed already interminable for both Elizabeth and the children. Even though they had more work than they could keep up with and seldom had time to dwell on Nathan's absence, the entire situation was wretched for all of them.

Hannah and Nate – the twins – had each other as had always

been the case since birth, but Gracie and Samuel seemed lost. Gracie had just turned thirteen, and Samuel, the oldest, turned fourteen and had been almost old enough to join the militia, but he was needed at home more than on the battlefield. Elizabeth could not have stood it if he had left with his father. He was old enough to be "man of the house" and stepped in where his father had left off. Everyone was trying to embody the spirit of independence with as much courage as possible.

Also helping with everything on the farm were the grown girls – Eunice, Asia, Sarah, Ruth, Mary, and Betty – with their husbands. Normally, the sons-in-law farmed the forty acres of land with Nathan, and the girls took care of duties, such as milking the cows, tending the chickens, making butter, and taking care of the vegetable gardens. However, now it was not unusual to see one of the girls helping plow the fields, detassel the corn, or harvest hay.

Unbeknownst to the husbands of the sisters, they would be called into duty by winter. The six men, who felt good about serving their country, still were dismayed about leaving their wives and small children. However, the Hoyt girls all bonded together to withstand not only the heartaches but also the tribulations of being alone. Afterall, every other wife in the thirteen colonies was in the same boat with maybe even more afflictions to face than the Hoyts.

Samuel spent most mornings hunting deer, rabbits, and squirrels with Beauty, his two-year-old spaniel, and on this particular day, he returned with six rabbits and three squirrels, which Elizabeth shared with the other families.

"Children, I need you to clean the rabbits and squirrels," declared Elizabeth, as she went out the door to tend to the vegetable garden. "If I'm not back when you finish, then put the rabbits and squirrels on to roast."

Samuel entered the house as his mother exited, and he quickly motioned to his brother and sisters.

"I have something special," Samuel whispered. "When I was hunting today, I came upon a stray spaniel. He and Beauty took to each other, and I put Beauty and him in the barn for now. I need to break this news to Ma with the hope that she will let us keep him."

"Oh, can I go see him?" asked Grace.

"No, no, we can't go to the barn right now because we will arouse suspicion with Ma. Wait until we sit down to eat," responded Samuel, "and I'll bring up the subject."

"What color is he?" continued Grace.

"He is black and tan and totally different from Beauty."

* * * *

Hannah had the rabbits and squirrels on the spits to roast when Elizabeth came in from gardening. Samuel and Nate were outside tending the cows and chickens when they were called for supper. There was excitement in the air, which Elizabeth was too tired to notice.

Hannah said the table prayer, and the food was passed.

"This smells wonderful, girls. You are becoming quite the cooks," Elizabeth commented.

The children were eyeing each other, waiting for Samuel to begin his story.

"Ma, I have something to ask you," Samuel began slowly. "While Beauty and I were hunting today, I came upon a stray spaniel. He has not been trained well, so I think that someone dropped him off and left him as a pup. It's very sad because he has been neglected, and you know how much I love dogs. I hate to see that happen to any animal." Samuel continued without a breath so that he could deliver all of his thoughts before his mother could speak. "Could we please keep him? He's very handsome – black and tan."

"So this is why all of you have been so quiet. Well, I don't know, Samuel. Has everyone seen this dog except for me?"

"No, only Nate who was helping me in the barn," responded Samuel.

"He's a great looking dog, Ma," chimed in Nate. "Please, please, please."

Elizabeth smiled. Of the two parents, she was more easily won over.

"We'll see after we eat. Now is not the time."

The children eyed each other, but they kept their thoughts concerning the dogs to themselves for the time being. Conversation centered around the war as was usual at the table.

"What did Pa say in his letter?" Nate questioned.

"He said that he had the honor of meeting General Henry Knox who brought the artillery down to Boston from Fort Ticonderoga. Do you remember that?"

"Oh, yes!" exclaimed Hannah and Nate in unison.

They were familiar with much of the Patriots' activities as the war was usually the main topic of conversation in any gathering.

"Pa and Job got to meet him?" questioned Gracie.

Elizabeth nodded. "Your Pa actually had the opportunity to sit and talk with General Knox. He really enjoyed getting to know the general a little. Knox told them about his life outside of the military.

"Also, your Pa talked about how kind farmers' wives have been to Job and him when they have had to ask for food. All in all, they are still trying to get to Philadelphia," Elizabeth concluded.

"Ma, do you think that I should enlist?" asked Samuel.

"No, son. You're too young to start with, and what would we do without you here to help? We've got an entire farm to run, and your help is essential. We'll talk more about it when you become of age," concluded Elizabeth, who hoped the idea would be forgotten by then. Besides, Samuel had one leg that was a bit lame from a farm accident the previous year. She was hoping it was enough to keep him out of the military when he turned sixteen.

It was dark by the time Samuel was allowed to bring both Beauty and the stray into the house for inspection. The new dog was dirty from roaming in the woods for who knew how long, but Samuel was correct that he was a handsome animal.

"I can use more help in hunting, Ma. What do you say?" said Samuel.

Elizabeth loved animals, and she immediately started petting the stray. "Hannah, bring me the brush."

Elizabeth spent the next fifteen minutes brushing the spaniel, who had tangles everywhere on his body. All the while, Elizabeth was talking softly to the dog, and the children eyed each other and smiled.

Meanwhile, Samuel was gathering table scraps to feed both Beauty and the stray, who gobbled everything in sight.

"Put him in the barn for tonight, and tomorrow you clean him up. Perhaps he can stay."

With a yelp from the children, Elizabeth was given hugs and kisses from everyone who assumed that "perhaps" was a "yes." They were correct.

* * * *

Some weeks later, Samuel had to go into Lexington to gather some cooking supplies needed by his mother. The town was in bedlam, and to start, Samuel was fearful something horrendous had happened in the war.

Samuel rushed into the Stone's General Store. "Mr. Stone, what is happening. What is all of this uproar in the streets?"

"Haven't you heard, Samuel? Two days ago, Philadelphia had a crisis meeting of the Continental Congress. The committee wanted to declare total independence from Britain, which would mean the birth of democracy for the colonies.

"Well, it has happened, and today they ratified a document that will change us forever. It's called 'The Declaration of Independence.' Briefly, it states that all men are created equal, and that our rights do not come from the king or government. Rather, our rights come from God, and they can't be taken away."

"What!" exclaimed Samuel. "Isn't that treason?"

"Indeed, it could be called that," responded Mr. Stone, "but we're on the cusp of something great. This is the start of the United States of America."

Everyone was in the streets shouting, laughing, cheering, singing, and blowing horns. It was a glorious time for celebration, and the people no longer wanted to be called "colonists" but rather "Americans."

Samuel quickly did the shopping for his mother and then went directly home to relay the news to the family.

"People are in a fracas in Lexington, Ma," remarked Samuel, out of breath from running all the way home. "You need to go into town to see it. I've never seen anything like it. People are singing, dancing, and cheering in the streets. The Continental Congress has adopted something called 'The Declaration of Independence' – freedom from Britain."

"Oh, please, can we go, Ma?" asked Hannah.

"I've never heard of such a thing. Everyone is out in the streets of Lexington, you say?" questioned Elizabeth.

Samuel nodded.

"Well, do you think that it's safe for the children to go?"

"Oh, I believe it's safe, Ma. People are just so joyous – just happily celebrating. I think that it's something that all of us should see. I believe that it's a momentous time for our country," responded Samuel.

"All right, then, children. Let's finish putting these supplies away and see what is so wonderful in Lexington that they have to take to the streets to celebrate," replied Elizabeth with a smile. "What is today's date?"

"It's the fourth of July, Ma," responded Samuel.

"Captain Benjamin Tallmadge and his son William"
by Ralph Earl

CHAPTER 5

CAPTAIN BENJAMIN TALLMADGE AND LIEUTENANT NATHAN HOYT

Job and Nathan Hoyt never made it to Philadelphia. Job came into contact with a friend from Lexington, Caleb Jones, who told him that Job and Anna's baby, Maria, had died.

"From what Anna said, she got sick one night with a fever and just couldn't recover. The doctor did several visits with no success. I'm so sorry, Job," Caleb stated.

The shock of the news was overwhelming, and Job put his head into his hands and sobbed quietly. Nathan tried to console him, but he was too devastated himself to be a comfort to Job.

Eventually, Job threw down his rifle. "I need to be with my family now," he declared as he packed his knapsack. "I need to let my heart heal."

His father didn't want to tell him that a man's heart never would heal fully from the death of a child, but Nathan hugged his son and wished him the best in the journey back to Lexington.

Job teamed up with a troop heading north as it wasn't safe to travel alone. Nathan later found out that one of the soldiers in the troop had recently lost a child, and the two of them comforted each other on the northward trek.

When Nathan Hoyt finally reached the northwestern edge of New York state, he embraced a group of gallant, strong-willed men. Although they were shabbily dressed and underfed, they were a friendly group who enjoyed joking and laughing, which was just what Nathan needed.

"We are aiming to join forces with General George Washington," commented one of the young soldiers who looked to be about seventeen. "We think that he is about forty miles away, and we'll make good time." The young man smiled. "Do you want to join us, Mr. Hoyt?"

"Please, call me Nathan, and I didn't get your name."

"It's Jeremiah Pitchford. I come from the Lake Champlain area."

"You're a long way from home, son."

"Yes, but some of these men here are my uncles, so I'll be well taken care of," responded Pitchford, slapping one of his uncles on his back.

"I'd be honored to join your group," asserted Hoyt. "Thank you."

Even though the group were not well dressed, Nathan was entranced by the spirit and courage of the soldiers.

That evening, Pitchford told Hoyt a story. "Several weeks ago, we witnessed a ghastly sight – a soldier had been caught and executed for desertion to the enemy. The ground on which the gallows were erected had been previously used for several other hangings.

"We soldiers were paraded passed the executed deserter to impress on us the need to preserve our allegiance to the American army," stated Pitchford. "It was a very unpleasant experience but one that we won't forget."

"Where are these other soldiers?" Hoyt asked.

"We left them as our aim was finding General Washington. The others headed north," Pitchford remarked.

It was July 4, 1776, and unbeknownst to the soldiers at the time, Congress had just adopted the Declaration of Independence. Congress had named a five-man committee to prepare a declaration, but it was up to the brilliant 33-year-old Thomas Jefferson to write the first draft alone in his rented room in Philadelphia. The declaration then went through a series of revisions made by Congress, and, finally, on July 4, 1776, Congress adopted Jefferson's revised Declaration of Independence.

The colonists now had committed the most outrageous act of treason. Congress knew the risks – death by hanging, poverty, dishonor for their families – and yet they signed. The United States of America was officially formed!

A few Americans recoiled from the Declaration of Independence, but the majority of the street crowds showed no restraint. Everywhere, until the last frontier settlement got the news in September, communities were persistent with their festivities.

On July 9, General Washington ordered that all Patriot armies be read the "Declaration of Independence":

"We hold these truths to be self-evident, that all men are created equal, that they are endowed by their Creator with certain unalienable Rights, that among these are Life, Liberty and the pursuit of Happiness…. And for the support of this Declaration, with a firm reliance on the protection of Divine Providence, we mutually pledge to each other our Lives, our Fortunes, and our sacred Honor."

＊ ＊ ＊ ＊

Hoyt was amazed and honored to meet General George Washington when he and the small group of soldiers caught up with Washington's platoon. It was July 9, and everyone was given the opportunity to hear the reading of the Declaration of Independence by Washington himself.

Silence was maintained as Washington read, but at the con-clusion, the soldiers exploded in a frenzy in commemoration of this important time in history.

Hoyt curiously watched Washington from a distance. At the age of forty-four, Washington was a tall, imposing figure. His hair re-mained light brown, and – except for formal occasions – he didn't powder it. He combed it straight back and tied it in a ponytail, a conventional style for the time. His eyes were a striking blue, and he was fair skinned. Being such a powerful, prominent figure in middle age, Nathan attempted to imagine him twenty years earlier.

In the first days after Hoyt arrived, he heard rumors that the troops were in training for an eventual siege on New York City. Never would Hoyt have imagined Washington's troops to be such an undisciplined, ragtag group of soldiers. He had expected Washington's men to be trained and admirable. Thus, much training would be needed to make the soldiers fit to fight the British in New York City.

Little did Hoyt know that Washington himself had been shocked when he first arrived from Mount Vernon and saw the shabbily dressed, disheveled soldiers who were to be his troop. With no formal training, they seemed to Washington to be un-ruly and unregimented.

Ever a stoic man, Washington had never despaired over a slightly ill-equipped army; however, this totally untrained group of soldiers was unexpected even to him. Washington tried to fortify his thoughts with the fact that the soldiers all had to have been strengthened by the backbreaking duties that they had en-dured in the colonies before the war.

It was at this point that Washington attained some command-ers who had been trained in Philadelphia, and they helped to bring the troops up to par. By August, the troops seemed stronger in their endeavors, and, without a doubt, they were faithful to their cause.

By late summer, Washington announced to the troops, "Unexpectedly, last week, some Patriots have secretly made their way into New York City, and, under the veil of darkness, have torn down the statue of King George III. The lead statue has been melted into 42,000 musket balls. It was a miraculous act when it occurred, but right now it wouldn't be possible at all. New York harbor is growing white with British sails, and Redcoats and Hessians are on the ground, ready to fight."

James Hawthorne, one of Washington's soldiers, was good at picking up all sorts of off-handed bits of information which normally turned out to be true. He stated one day to Hoyt, "I heard one of the commanders say that the general is ready to lead us into Manhattan and win New York City. However, I also heard that there are no spies for General Washington yet, so he doesn't know the number of men in General William Howe's army."

"That could be a possible problem. I guess that we are going to have to trust Washington and hope that his decisions are favorable. There will be times, I'm sure, that we'll have to learn from our mistakes," concluded Hoyt, who tried to remain optimistic.

As it turned out, Hawthorne's information was true. Washington, unfortunately, marched his 10,000 men into Redcoat territory with their troops numbering 20,000 British and 30,000 mercenary German troops.

Washington found himself essentially trapped by the British and Germans in Brooklyn Heights with no way to escape. Just like that, the Revolutionary War could have been over!

Washington could have thought that the colonists had no chance against the mighty King of England, who held the strongest empire in the world. Again, though, Washington never lost his nerve in battle. Fortunately, nothing seemed to shake his determination.

Thus, as evening fell on August 29, 1776, with the Patriots trapped, Washington knew his only escape from Brooklyn Heights was by water. Even that evasion would take a miracle.

With a hasty retreat projected, Washington had chosen to evacuate in the dark of night. With only ten flat-bottomed boats on hand, the army – along with every horse and every piece of artillery – was ferried across the water.

To Washington's relief, the British troops didn't spot the shadowy silhouettes of escaping Patriots under the cover of darkness. However, as the sky lightened with the dawn, there were still some men to move. Fortunately, a thick fog rolled in that allowed all the Patriots to attain safety.

Much to Washington's chagrin, the Patriots had lost New York City, but – on the bright side – he had saved the new nation's army.

In a meeting that Washington had with the commanders of the troops, he divulged, "I'm afraid that we won't always be able to beat the Redcoats with manpower, arms, or force. We are going to have to use our senses, brains, and wits. We are going to need to intelligently outmaneuver – not physically overpower– the enemy."

The troops were confused with Washington's message. However, Washington was implying that spies would play a crucial role in the outcome of the war. The general needed a spy ring that couldn't be broken.

With that thought foremost in his mind, Washington immediately commenced to establish a flawless spy ring. To begin, he needed one good man. He began to narrow down a list of trustworthy and organized men whom he knew well, so that only one remained in the end.

* * * *

In the beginning phases of the war, Washington, unfortunately, lost many battles. For all of Washington's virtues, he was neither a professional soldier nor the product of a military academy. Most of his adult life had been spent in farming and surveying. His only prior experience in the army had been to command a small provincial army.

Washington seemed to be reborn, though, because of his present as well as his past tribulations in the war. December 25, 1777, was a night to be remembered for Washington's army. There were 1,500 Germans under Colonel Johann Rall holding Trenton, New Jersey, on that Christmas Day Eve. Unknown to the British, Washington had placed a spy in the Redcoats' army, who had led Colonel Rall to believe that the Continental Army was exhausted and disheartened with no plans of advancing on them.

Therefore, the Redcoats and Hessians celebrated Christmas to the fullest with much drink, and Washington decided to attack. On this one military exploit, Washington was risking half of his army, all of his hope, and the future of the United States of America. However, Washington was stalwart as always, and the password for this battle was "Victory or Death."

December 25 was fearfully cold and raw with a snowstorm brewing. It was a terrible night for Washington's soldiers, many with no shoes or just rags tied around their frostbitten feet. A person could easily have followed the tracks of the Patriots because the road was covered in blood.

In the late hours of December 25 and the early hours of December 26, Washington's soldiers took boats over the Delaware River. It was 8:00 in the morning of December 26 when the last of the soldiers finally arrived on the Trenton shore.

"I'm afraid that we're too late," alleged Hoyt's friend, Thomas Franklin. "We're hours behind because of the storm, and Washington wanted a surprise attack."

"Yes, we've possibly lost the element of surprise at daybreak," admitted Hoyt, "but let's not be dispirited. General Washington standing there on the shore looks more determined than ever. We can't let him down."

Washington was concerned that there could possibly be a few Germans on guard; however, the Germans believed that the Americans weren't going to attack; besides, no one in his right mind would be out in a snowstorm like the one they were experiencing. In the end, the storm was a godsend for the Patriots as it totally covered their approach.

The Germans had all been feasting and drinking and were now sleeping off their party when the Americans entered on both ends of Trenton. Escape was cut off. The enemy troops surrendered when Colonel Rall was killed, and the Americans took 1,000 prisoners and 40 horses. Amazingly, not one American died.

On the last day of December, Washington's men again crossed the Delaware River toward Princeton, and on January 3, the Patriots stood strong, taking most of New Jersey. Franklin and Hoyt both noticed that the greatest prize of this battle was the American morale skyrocketing. The Americans had discovered a newfound strength in their victories. This was definitely the turning point of the war.

* * * *

By now Nathan Hoyt had been promoted to the status of Lieutenant Nathan Hoyt because of his skills, keenness of mind, courage, gallantry, and trustworthiness. Washington had spotted Hoyt early on – he stood out as an asset to a spy ring.

In fact, Washington had nearly picked Hoyt for the spying task that he awarded to Captain Nathan Hale. Venturing behind enemy lines disguised as a Loyalist, Hale was to investigate the Loyalists' movements and report back to Washington so that New York City could be regained.

Hale was to sneak into New York City by making his way to Connecticut, cross the Sound, and land on Long Island behind the British encampments. He was then to make his way to Brooklyn.

Hale would pose as a schoolmaster looking for work, a cover that would give him an excuse to meet leading townsmen and ask questions about the area.

On September 21, Washington spent most of the day making potential battle plans. He was unaware that at that moment, Nathan Hale was being arrested, charged with espionage, and sentenced to "be hanged by the neck until dead."

Nathan Hale stood resolute and courageous to the very end, pledging in his last moments alive, "I only regret that I have but one life to lose for my country."

However, by now, Washington had a plan to form an entire spy ring. From the list of men that he had narrowed down, Washington came up with Captain Benjamin Tallmadge, who had gone to Yale and had been a friend of Hale's.

"Captain Tallmadge, you have already proved yourself to be a diligent soldier in Connecticut's Continental Army," acknowledged General Washington to Tallmadge, who had been called into the general's office, "and you've been devoted to training your men for scouting missions and performing raids. I need to organize an undisputed, highly disciplined spy ring. You're the first person that I've asked to join this ring, and, in addition, I'd like you to head up this spy ring."

Nathan Hale spying on the Redcoats

Tallmadge was stunned. Washington's sanction rendered him almost speechless. He sat for a few moments with his hands clasped in his lap.

Finally, he divulged his thoughts. "Thank you, General, for your kind words. You know, my older brother, William, was captured by the British and died on one of their prison boats. He was dreadfully mistreated as were all of the American prisoners.

"My brother's death has made my commitment to the Patriot cause more personal, and I am honored to become the first to be asked into this spy ring. In addition, I accept with full continuity the role of leader of the ring."

Nathan Hoyt was not yet aware of any spy ring, and even if he had been, he couldn't have shared any of that information with his family. However, he had other news to share in his letter home.

Washington crossing the Delaware

CHAPTER 6

LETTER FROM NATHAN AND AT HOME IN LEXINGTON

Dearest Elizabeth

We have received – from Caleb Jones – the heart-wrenching news of Maria. Tears flowed unceasingly from both of us. It was almost too much for our son to handle, and he threw in his rifle and headed home-ward. Whether he has reached home yet or not, I don't know. I am praying for his safe return. Godspeed to our poor daughter-in-law, Anna. I don't know if I can feel her sorrow, but I do know my own.

I must tell you one speck of good news that has happened. First off, I have had the privilege of meeting the great General George Washington. His stature is well over six feet, and we all feel diminished in his presence. We don't see him smile much, but he has such a burden to bear as the general in charge of the American armies.

Soldiers have told me previously that Washington is a cold person. However, I had the honor of sitting with him briefly the first night that I reached camp, and he came off as friendly and caring. He even asked about my journey.

Secondly, I must report to you that yesterday I was promoted to lieutenant. No longer am I Private Nathan Hoyt. General Washington said that in the short time that he has known and supervised me, I have excelled. I feel so honored. Again, I don't find anything "cold" about the general. A personable individual gives compliments, and that's how I see Washington.

I know that you have by now had the privilege of reading or hearing the Declaration of Independence that was written during the summer. What an incredible document! General Washington read it to us on July 9, and we were all so taken by its greatness. Even though it has been said by our commanders that "these are the times that try men's souls," I also see extraordinary things – as the Declaration of Independence – coming out of these times.

As you can well imagine, we are seeing horrible things right now, because of battles and death. But if we can gain independence, it will all have been well worth it. No longer will Britain drain us with all of the taxes on their products, and we as an independent nation can make our own decisions. We will not have to bow to the king's decisions and rules.

I want to tell you about something that seemed somewhat of a miracle the night that it happened. This occurred one night under Washington's command when we were setting up our huts for future cold months. It was a show of northern lights in the heavens; or, at least, it was how we imagined the northern lights to look. The whole visible sky appeared to be lit, and it looked like crimson velvet. No one had ever seen such a spectacle, and it helped boost our morale that night simply because it was such a beautiful, heavenly phenomenon.

I must tell you of one battle that was a huge success for us. We had set up camp near the Delaware River, and our commanding officer said to us, "Now, men, you have been wishing for days to fight the British. By tomorrow morning, you will have had such a chance to fight."

This did so much to raise our courage, and even the wounded and sick men begged to go on the mission. Of course, they were denied, but all of us who were able to fight were ready.

I'll tell you briefly what happened. It was Christmas night, and General Washington took us over the Delaware River, and we made our way towards Trenton, New Jersey, and General Rall's troops. It was fearfully cold and raw with a huge snowstorm. It turned out to be a terrible night for some of the soldiers who had no shoes and ragged clothing. I was more fortunate, though.

The Redcoats and Hessians were sleeping off their celebration of Christmas. As we arrived near Trenton, Lieutenant Rall was shot and was mortally wounded. The Redcoats and Hessians surrendered.

We learned later that, ironically, Lieutenant Rall had been playing cards that night. Apparently, the Germans had had a spy among our Continental Army, and the spy had delivered a note to Rall saying that the Americans were planning an attack. Rall didn't read it but rather put it into his pocket. It was found by one of our army while recovering Rall's body.

One of the British prisoners we took confirmed the story. It was a remarkable victory for us.

With the storm still raging on December 26 and 27, Washington decided to wait until the next day to make the return trip over the river. December 29 would be just two days before enlisted men could leave his army. Of course, Washington was praying none of them would depart.

The general normally avoided an oratory, but now he made a personal appeal to the enlisted men, urging them to stay. Something in the plea struck the hearts of the enlisted men, and nearly all the men stepped forward to continue their enlistment.

I must close this letter because tomorrow I hope to find someone to drop it at the postal service. I pray every night that all of you are well. Know that you are continually loved.

Your devoted husband,
Nathan

* * * *

The day after Maria died, Elizabeth was telling a friend – Caroline, who lived in Lexington – of the unfortunate story.

"Little Maria had become ill one night soon before bed. Anna stayed next to Maria all night because of the coughing and runny nose, and when the fever started and quickly spiked the next morning, she sent for a doctor. A neighbor was sent to beckon me.

"By the time I got there, Anna had put Maria into a cool tub of water, but the fever continued. The doctor arrived and spent half an hour with Maria in an attempt to diagnose the sickness. Doctor Bland asked if Maria had had any chills, but Anna didn't know of any. The doctor reported that it could be diphtheria or possibly pneumonia. She definitely had congestion in her lungs."

"Oh, a death warrant," asserted Caroline. "I'm so sorry, Elizabeth."

Elizabeth was dabbing her eyes. Obviously, it was a difficult story to tell.

"Dr. Bland handed Anna some herbs, directing her to make the herbs into a poultice and put it on Maria's chest," continued Elizabeth. "Sadly, it was all that he could do. Maria died the next day after a second visit by the doctor.

"Obviously, we were all devastated, and her sisters-in-law, Ruth and Betty, both tried to console Anna. My daughter Betty had lost a son to a farming accident two years previously, and she understood the grief. However, Anna was inconsolable," concluded Elizabeth.

It was at times like these that the sisters missed their husbands the most. The men had all, by now, had to enlist and had been gone for several months. The sisters got letters infrequently – one or two a year – and they prayed that their husbands were all safe, but everyone knew that the soldiers were underfed and cold. Four of the husbands were in the Quebec region and the other two were in the Virginia area. God listened to many prayers from the Hoyt girls during the war.

* * * *

The spaniel stayed, and after much deliberation, the children named him Trusty. Samuel took him hunting nearly every day, and Trusty's training went well. He and Beauty were best friends, and they were continually together – during the day and at night.

Trusty was carefully watching Beauty's expert hunting techniques, and he was a fast learner. He was able to retrieve the rabbit or squirrel nearly as well and fast as Beauty. The children could see Trusty's pride as he trotted back with his retrieved animal. Samuel had never tried pheasant hunting, but he was now considering it with two dogs to help him in his expeditions.

One morning, Elizabeth commented to the children at breakfast, "I think that Beauty is going to have puppies."

The children looked at each other in shock.

"Do you really believe that?" asked Gracie.

"Yes. Have you noticed that she is bulging a bit in the stomach?" continued Elizabeth.

"Yes, but I thought that she had just gained weight," responded Gracie.

"That would be impossible," proclaimed Samuel. "We don't have much food to feed the dogs."

"How will we be able to feed puppies?" questioned Hannah.

"The problem will be finding more food for Beauty because the puppies will be nursing. It's another bridge that we'll cross when we come to it," confessed Elizabeth. "God will provide."

Fall had arrived and with it came school for the children. If the parent wanted to send the children, it had been decided in Lexington that the schooling would be only half a day, starting at noon and extending until four in the afternoon. This solution would allow the children to help with all of the morning chores.

Elizabeth had already made up her mind that the children would continue to attend school even though the extra work would be a consequence for her. Elizabeth had ten grandchildren, some of whom were old enough to be in school as well. Her older daughters were also intent on keeping their children in school, attending to the extra work themselves. How? They weren't sure at the moment, but, again, it was one day at a time.

Two of Elizabeth's older children, Eunice and Sarah, said that they would come and attend to some of the chores to make their mother's life a bit easier. Harvesting was fast approaching, and the ladies were going to be in charge of that project plus all of the duties at home.

The fall had been cold, damp, and rainy – a bit unusual for New England – and the women were concerned about how they would accomplish the task of harvesting with the drizzle continuing day after day.

"We needed some of this rain this summer when there were weeks of drought," declared Eunice one day as they canned some of the vegetables from the garden.

There had been a good harvest of garden vegetables – green beans, beets, cucumbers, carrots, and potatoes. Everything was being canned. Apples from the numerous apple trees on their property were ample, and the making of jelly was also underway.

Elizabeth nodded. "However, God has been good to us in so many ways since your father and your husbands left, and we must not complain."

After all of the work for the day had been completed, Elizabeth would spend time reading in the Bible to the children. Often, if they weren't too tired, Elizabeth would also read a story from one of the classics – which Nathan was proud to own – on the bookshelf near the fireplace.

* * * *

It was at this time that a new emigrant family – the McDonalds – from Ireland moved in down the road. The house had been owned by the Walsh family, and it became vacant when the husband and son left for the war, and the wife moved to Concord to be with her ailing parents.

Sean and Violet McDonald along with their ten-year-old daughter, Patsy, soon became good friends with the Hoyts. While in Ireland, the McDonalds had lost two children to smallpox, and they wanted a new start in a different country. Coming to America in the spring – before the war had started – and settling in New York had been both a privilege and a mistake.

They had made friends quickly and seemed to fit well into the community, so that was a plus. However, the soil in the area of New York in which they settled was not rich and fertile, and their crops failed for two years. With a cousin in Lexington who told them of the lush, abundant soil in Massachusetts, the McDonalds made the decision to move.

"We're so glad that we moved," commented Violet. "Farming is so much better here, and we love our neighbors and the town of Lexington. You would think that we are all relatives of the people whom we have met. And Patsy so enjoys the company of your girls. All of you have been so gracious to her."

"We love Patsy," Hannah declared. "She has so many different ideas from what we have. Gracie and I are going to go to Ireland someday!"

That brought a laugh from all of them.

"Be sure to let Patsy know because she would love to show you around and have you meet all of her friends in Dublin," responded Violet, still laughing.

Elizabeth smiled. "It's so good that your family moved so close to us because when school is done in the afternoon and the children's chores are finished, it's wonderful that Patsy can come and play."

Elizabeth, too, had found a friend in Violet. Always generous, sweet, and sharing, Violet seemed to make life a little better for Elizabeth, who became depressed from time to time with so much work as well as concern about Nathan.

"Will Sean have to join the militia?" asked Elizabeth when the conversation seemed to come to a standstill.

"We don't know for sure. Right now, we are considered Irish, which is neither English nor American. Sean may not be asked to go to war. However, we consider ourselves Americans now, and Sean possibly will want to serve his nearly-acquired country."

Top: Abraham Woodhull.
Bottom: Marquis de Lafayette

CHAPTER 7

MARQUIS DE LAFAYETTE AND ABRAHAM WOODHULL

It was in July 1777 that Marquis de Lafayette arrived on the shores of America feeling the ill effects of not taking naturally to the sea. Having never been sea-born before, Lafayette hadn't relished his first experience.

"I'm going to have to become an American because I don't want to go through the journey back to France." Lafayette stated with a smile as he talked to the captain of the vessel. "It was a truly terrible experience."

Stepping into the post of General Washington after his first week in America, he was awed at the stature of Washington. Never having seen anyone so tall and muscular, Lafayette stood silently for a few moments before he extended his hand.

Washington clasped Lafayette's hand warmly. "Welcome to America, Marquis de Lafayette. It is such a pleasure to meet you. Your reputation precedes you to this country. Benjamin Franklin has spoken highly of you." Washington paused for a moment. "I heard that you had a difficult trip on the sea."

"Yes, indeed, you could say that. At least I was not the only one sick. My shipmates shared the same suffering," Lafayette said in his beautifully accented English. The soldiers found that

Lafayette had a tendency to express himself in language that was charming and with an accent that was alluring no matter the occasion.

Even as the two men were just formally meeting, Washington immediately achieved the status of an idol to the fatherless Lafayette. The marquis was very much attuned to becoming a part of the American military and insisted that he wanted to be placed in command of a division. Washington didn't immediately reply to the latter statement, wanting to get to know Lafayette first and view for himself the marquis' qualifications. In addition, being only nineteen years of age, Lafayette was virtually devoid of command experience, and, of course, Washington questioned his ability to lead as well as a seasoned commander. Washington left Lafayette's request hanging without an answer.

Over the next few months, Washington began to see in Lafayette the son that he had never had. Courageous, tactful, trustworthy, and ready to fight at a moment's notice, Lafayette soon acquired high esteem in Washington's eyes, and the bond with Lafayette grew.

In September 1777 Lafayette was injured in his first battle – the Battle of Brandywine. General William Howe shot Lafayette from behind. As it turned out, Lafayette's wound did him more good than harm because it was after surgery in the military hospital that Lafayette had the opportunity to become acquainted with many soldiers, nurses, and doctors. Being savvy and charismatic, Lafayette totally intrigued everyone with his personality plus the fact that he had come such a long distance to fight with the colonists in America.

While still confined to bed, Lafayette could do little more than read and write. And write he did. He drafted letter after letter to military personnel on both sides of the Atlantic. With scores of ideas on how to stop the English, Lafayette became a prime intermediary between America and France. In addition, because of Lafayette's comprehension of military knowledge and his close affiliation with the troops, Washington chose to make Lafayette his personal aide.

It was at this time that Alexander Hamilton also arrived on the scene. Washington saw the military skills of Hamilton during the horrific Trenton battle when the troops had to go to Trenton and return by way of the Delaware River, and he was impressed with Hamilton's skills. However, illness often kept Hamilton in the army hospital, and Washington decided to make not only Lafayette but also Hamilton his aide-de-Camp. Lafayette and Hamilton quickly bonded not only because they were both foreigners and orphans but also because they both spoke French.

* * * *

As the deathly cold of December bore down upon the army, General Washington sat in his hut at Valley Forge, and he couldn't help but notice the persistently poor condition of his troops.

Sitting with his eyes downcast, Washington spoke to Lieutenant Hoyt, who had entered to deliver a message from Tallmadge.

"At least a fifth of my men have no shoes. There are no blankets for some of the men, not enough food, and snow is everywhere. I had been told there would be eight months of food; in reality, there was only eight days' worth of supplies." Washington paused. "I feel guilty going out to talk with them. I'm fully clothed, warm, and adequately fed. Even the horses are dying from lack of forage. There must be money someplace in Philadelphia to equip these men. They haven't even been paid."

It was true that the snow-covered ground did hinder the

transport of food and military equipment; however, it was atrocious that there were times when the troops went days without eating anything of substance. In addition, living in constricted and unsanitary conditions was troublesome to the men's health. Indeed, it was times like these that Washington questioned if he was really the right man for this job.

Washington understood why men deserted the military, but the ones who stayed with him honored and respected him and knew they would eventually get paid. They believed in Washington, and Washington believed in the cause, which was independence from England. Thus, the general focused on keeping the Continental Army's spirit alive even in the darkest moments that seemed to consume everyone from time to time.

"Just as pathetic as the troops' environment, lack of food, and their clothing," stated Hoyt, "is the smallpox that has crept into the camp. So many men are dying from it."

"I know, and I hate to hear of it," responded Washington.

"There is a light at the end of the tunnel, though," remarked Hoyt.

The general raised his eyebrows in question.

"Doctor Waldo is developing something that seems to be working. He's calling it a vaccine – something not used before. He's taking pus from soldiers who are experiencing smallpox and spreading it on cuts of soldiers who are still well. It seems that they are then immune, and they are not contracting the disease."

General Washington sat with a hopeful light in his eyes, pondering the statement.

"Wonderful. Actually, ingenious," Washington finally stated. He had contracted the dreadful disease himself as a child and knew firsthand of its adversity.

"Getting back to our military business," Washington interrupted, "Benjamin Franklin has been in France, as you know. He's attempting to ally France to us Patriots, telling the French of our need of engineers, map makers, and soldiers skilled in military arts. As usual, Franklin – with his refinement and charm – is winning the faith of the French.

"I believe that you've probably already met the nineteen-year-old Marquis de Lafayette who is in our unit. Franklin brags of him as being an amiable, young nobleman who is intelligent as well as alluring. I actually have heard all of that also from the nurses and doctors who cared for him after his injury at Brandywine."

"Actually, I haven't had the opportunity to meet the marquis yet, but it will be an honor, I assure you," declared Hoyt.

Looking at his timepiece, Hoyt added, "Please don't think me rude, General, but I have work to do with my soldiers, so I must depart."

"One more thing that I want to tell you, Lieutenant, before you depart. Last night, I heard some exciting news. Philadelphia has adopted a thirteen-star flag for our newly named United States of America." Washington's face was beaming.

"I heard as much just this morning," Hoyt replied, a smile also brightening his face. "It's a very bright spot in this cold, gloomy winter day."

* * * *

It was during this dreary time at Valley Forge that a Prussian named Baron Friedrich von Steuben arrived. Although he was a Prussian nobleman, he was indeed an American sympathizer.

Understandably, von Steuben couldn't speak English well, so each night he would write out in German his next day's orders for the troops, and his aide would translate the orders into

"Friedrich Wilhelm von Steuben" by
Charles Willson Peale

French, with a French-speaking American then translating it into English. This procedure occurred each night, no matter how long it took to accomplish.

As von Steuben looked over the suffering army, he concluded that no European army could have held together in such circumstances – poor lodging, filthy clothing, inferior cooking along with disease. The spirit of the Patriots was impressive. Von Steuben made it his most noteworthy goal to train the ragtag men of Valley Forge to respect discipline and order, plus assist them in regaining their health. In short, von Steuben urged as well as trained the Patriots to be members of a professional army.

The baron introduced the bayonet to the army and helped the Patriots to fight as a remarkably highly trained army. Up until now, those who actually had a bayonet used it more for roasting meat over the fire – when they had meat, that is – rather than using it in battle. A bedraggled, untrained, hungry army went into Valley Forge, but a fearless, fighting force emerged. A new professional pride was born. In short, it seemed von Steuben had created a miracle.

Von Steuben's expertise with the troops was about to pay off at the Battle of Monmouth, New Jersey. As Washington's troops approached the battle, they saw other Americans in retreat, scrambling on foot through muddy ravines and thickened woods. Literally, thousands of uniformed men with muskets slung over their shoulders were stumbling toward Washington's troops. General Washington met General Charles Lee also fleeing and angrily demanded an explanation. Washington, who seldom swore, lost his temper that day.

"We have a war to win, General Lee. Get back and don't stop until we win this damn battle," yelled Washington in rage.

"Sir, the Recoats have taken the field," yelled Lee.

"That's because you gave it to them, you pompous, silly ass!" responded Washington.

Lee started to protest, but the general stopped him.

"General Lee, you're relieved of command. Retire to the rear."

With that, Washington took command of the troops, ordering them to return onto the field.

"Stand fast, boys; stand fast!" Washington shouted. "Turn and meet your enemy. Our artillery will support you. Today, we will win. Today is our day!"

The troops cheered loudly, turning and sweeping across the meadow toward the advancing Redcoats. Fight or die – they knew that they would fight.

By then, Lee had slunk back away from the troops. That was General Lee's last battle.

It was because of von Steuben's military training of precision and valor that the British realized that they were fighting a different kind of army now. Never again would the Patriots be viewed as unprepared or inept. Their new expertise had been well learned thanks to von Steuben.

As Lee's men and Washington's troops faced the British back at Monmouth, the battle continued long into the afternoon. As it turned out, the biggest foe on the field that day was not the British but rather the sweltering heat. With over 100-degree temperatures, many men literally fell in their tracks from the heat. Others ended up dying of heat stroke.

"Where are the Molly Pitchers?" one man choked as he lay on the ground, a bullet through his leg. "Bring me some water," he gasped.

The Molly Pitcher – a woman volunteering to serve the troops, taking them water throughout the battle – rushed to help the injured man.

Molly Pitchers were essential to the troops because they not only delivered water to the soldiers who were fighting, but they also helped cook food and wash uniforms during the evening hours.

At times, it was more than just a Molly Pitcher helping out. In some of the troops, there were whole families – wives, children, and dogs. They not only did work, but also provided comfort, nursing skills, and companionship. The amazing part was that the families didn't complain about all of the discomforts, but rather focused and performed all of the duties asked of them.

As it turned out, this battle at Monmouth was the last northern battle to be fought. With British General Henry Clinton retreating during the night, the victory fell to the Patriots.

* * * *

Washington continued his work on his secret spy ring. His plan was to get some intelligent person into New York City and others to be messengers. In other words, Washington wanted a chain of agents stationed permanently in enemy territory.

Because Washington wanted someone in New York City, Tallmadge considered his close friend, Abraham Woodhull. Tallmadge and Woodhull shared officers' ideals and had been friends for years. General Washington – who had bonded with Tallmadge and trusted him fully – had said that he would acquiesce to Tallmadge's suggestions, so Tallmadge only had to get Woodhull to concur.

Woodhull listened to Tallmadge's explanation of the spy ring.

"Abraham, General Washington and I have discussed the fact that we need some intelligent person inside of New York City, and I am allowed to make that choice. You are my preference. There could possibly be a messenger between you and me, so you don't have to worry about getting intelligence to me." Tallmadge paused for a moment to let the information sink in. Finally, he asked, "What are your thoughts, Abraham?"

Abraham Woodhull's kinsman, General Nathan Woodhull, had recently been callously and needlessly murdered by the Loyalists, and Woodhull was ready to avenge his death. Woodhull – more ready than Tallmadge had expected – agreed with the plan.

"It'll work out well because I have an excuse to go from Setauket into New York City to gain information since my sister, Mary, lives in Manhattan. I'll have all the provisions I need including a warm meal, a place to stay, and a reason to be in the City. No one will suspect me of anything," Woodhull avowed.

Tallmadge heartily agreed. "It will be your job, Abraham, to gather information about the Redcoats – pertinent intelligence that Washington would need to win battles – and you'll send it across the Sound to Long Island. The data will land in my hands, and I'll spirit it away to Washington wherever he is camped. Already, I have a man in mind to help me get intelligence to the general."

"So may I hire a man myself whom I want to help me carry out the work? Someone to carry the information to you if I'm not leaving New York City proper immediately?" asked Woodhull.

"Yes, of course, Abraham. Keep in mind that Washington would want the work carried out by a person knowing the land, water, and residents – a local man, in other words."

"Who will know of this spy ring?"

"Only General Washington and myself need to know about your involvement," Tallmadge asserted. "And, of course, anyone that you hire."

"Why me, though?" questioned Woodhull. He suddenly seemed a bit nervous – and not without cause.

Tallmadge formulated his thoughts before he answered. "Well, Abraham, you have no wife or children waiting for you at home. You are acquainted with the countryside, know excellent places to pick up local gossip, and which roads are the most adequate to travel. You know – God forbid – the best escape routes. And, most importantly, I know that you believe in this war for the sake of American virtue."

Woodhull stood listening and finally nodded.

Tallmadge selected a code name for Woodhull – his name would be Samuel Culper. Tallmadge himself would be John Bolton. The groundwork was laid for the Ring to begin work.

Tallmadge and Woodhull were in place to begin turning the wheel that would steadily roll out the defeat of the British in New York. They would engulf themselves in their new Loyalist identities and leave their former American lives behind. The charade of being devoted to the Crown had begun.

Still, one more important person was needed to transfer information from Tallmadge to Washington – that man was Lieutenant Nathan Hoyt.

Hoyt could not, of course, tell his wife of his new position when he wrote home to Elizabeth.

Top: *"The March to Valley Forge" by William Trego*

Bottom: *Huts in Valley Forge*

CHAPTER 8

LETTER FROM NATHAN AND AT HOME IN LEXINGTON

Dearest Elizabeth,

We are now in Valley Forge, getting ready for winter. Valley Forge is not too far from Philadelphia, which has now been taken by the British. We have heard that it was their goal to take the capital, and they did.

Many of the soldiers here in Valley Forge are in a forlorn condition, and some are very disheartened. Let me quickly add that I am in better shape than many, and I will refer back to that in a moment.

For many, their condition is appalling, especially to us New Englanders who have not been accustomed to such hardships at home. But we are bound to defend our injured country and will persevere as long as hardships are not intolerable.

There is a special reason why my condition is better than some of the other soldiers. I have met a remarkable Frenchman whom I have had the privilege of befriending. His name is Marquis de Lafayette.

Almost as soon as he joined General Washington's troops, I believe that the general and the marquis formed a special bond. The general looks at the marquis as a father would his son. Since the general is childless, I believe that he feels a special affection for the marquis. In addition, I have heard that the marquis is fatherless, and I wonder if possibly he looks at Washington as a father figure. Thus, the bond is mutual.

The marquis was wounded in his first battle at the Battle of Brandywine and has been recuperating in the military hospital where I visit regularly to take supplies to the surgeons. I always stop to visit a bit with the marquis, and we discuss current military matters.

He has special supplies of food and clothing delivered to him, being the marquis and a privileged soldier in our troop. He often shares his belongings with me, and I feel very honored to have him as a friend.

I was not in the Battle of Brandywine in which my friend was injured. General Washington's troops had been divided, and I was left to help guard the encampment. At any rate, the fighting was so fierce that Philadelphians could hear the guns 25 miles away. As the sun went down, the Patriots had to declare defeat.

I also had the privilege of meeting a friend of Lafayette's, Alexander Hamilton. Even though he was orphaned at a young age in the West Indies, Hamilton is exceptionally personable and brilliant. Lafayette and Hamilton often speak French to each other, and, I must admit, it is a beautiful language.

And then, I met another European who has joined our ranks, Baron von Steuben. He speaks German so his English isn't fluent, but his presence is impressive. It seems that von Steuben also speaks French, so he often barks his commands to Hamilton who in turn shouts them in English to the troops. It can be almost comical.

It seems that von Steuben has been getting us more food and updating our worn-out clothing with warmer coats to help in the upcoming winter. He is also attempting to instill in General Washington's troops a new professional pride.

The last battle that our troops fought in was the Battle of Monmouth when the soldiers saw General Lee's troops retreating through the woods. General Washington was cursing, which was certainly unlike him because we soldiers have seldom heard such words from the general's mouth.

Anyway, he ordered the brigades to make a stand and ordered the artillery to secure the retreat. I was told that both the general as well as Alexander Hamilton were everywhere amid the soldiers, cheering them by voice and example and restoring the fight. Hamilton didn't stop until his horse was shot out from under him, and he collapsed from heat stroke.

Eventually, the Redcoats reluctantly crawled back and hid themselves from our sight. In the end, they retreated during the night, leaving our soldiers with the victory. We wish that all of our battles would end this way, and, I have to say, it was a complete morale booster to the troops.

I attempt not to talk about the battles; however, Monmouth was recent and a great victory for us Patriots, and I wanted you to share in the success.

As I lay awake some nights, my thoughts are continually on you, Elizabeth, and the children and grandchildren. Please be safe.

Your loving husband,
Nathan

* * * *

The puppies had been born the previous week, and the house had become filled with fun, laughter, and yipping. What precious little creatures they were. Beauty was protective and very motherly with her newly born brood.

With three females and two males, the children plus Patsy each had the opportunity to name one puppy. After much deliberation, the puppies were named Daphne, Jewel, Tulip, Captain, and Ranger. Beauty raced around making sure that any messes that the puppies made were cleaned up immediately, and then she lay lovingly to nurse her babies. Four of the puppies shared the tan and black colors; however, Daphne was pure black like Beauty.

"Are you sure that you don't mind if I take a puppy?" questioned Patsy one evening.

"You are welcome to one as long as your parents don't mind," declared Elizabeth.

"My parents say that they can't say no because I left all of my friends and relatives back in Ireland, and a puppy would help fulfill that hole. And, by the way, they are so grateful that I was able to befriend all of you," concluded Patsy as she looked from one to another of the Hoyt family.

"All of you have been wonderful to me. When we lived in New York, I cried all of the time because I missed Ireland and my friends. Life is different now because of all of you," Patsy remarked with a broad smile.

"We're the lucky ones to have you as our best friend, Patsy," stated Hannah, returning the smile.

"Which puppy do you want, Patsy?" inquired Gracie.

"I really love Jewel. She and I formed a bond as soon as she could walk."

"Perfect then," responded Elizabeth with a smile. "Jewel is yours."

* * * *

It was late one night when there was a knock at the door. Fearful of a caller after dark, Elizabeth put the children into the far back bedroom and went to the door with the rifle. There stood three Oneida Native Americans. Elizabeth recognized one as Little Bear, who had been Nathan's childhood friend.

"Please, come in out of the cold," stated Elizabeth.

The three stepped inside and waited for Elizabeth to pull up chairs for them. By then, they were surrounded by the puppies, who weren't tiny anymore.

The Native Americans sat with their faces blank until finally Elizabeth asked them, "What can I do for you, friends?"

"We need food," revealed Little Bear. "We have furs to trade with you for corn."

Thinking about the cold winters, Elizabeth knew that she could use the furs to make into clothing for the children.

"We have extra corn stored in the cellar," divulged Elizabeth. "Let me get the children, and Samuel can fetch some for you. We have had a good harvest so I will be grateful for the furs in exchange for the corn."

As Elizabeth exited the living quarters, the three Native Americans knelt down to cuddle the furry little creatures who were determined to make friends.

The children all had their ears plastered against the door when Elizabeth went to fetch them. Anxiously, they went into the living area to meet the Native Americans. They had, of course, met Little Bear, but no one was acquainted with the other two.

They soon learned that Little Bear was now called Chaska, which meant "first born son." The other two were Tala, meaning "wolf," and Kanga, meaning "black bird."

Elizabeth sent Samuel to gather some corn, and the other three children attempted to talk with their guests. Chaska pulled four small red feathers from his pouch and handed one to each of the children, saving one for Samuel when he returned from the cellar.

"For you for good luck, courage and strength," stated Chaska. "Keep in your pouch."

"But we don't have a pouch," responded Nate.

Chaska pointed to Nate's pocket, and Nate nodded with a smile.

The Native Americans were continually eyeing the puppies.

"Would you like to have a puppy?" asked Elizabeth as she walked from the kitchen with water to heat on the fire for tea.

Their eyes widened, and Chaska responded, "Yes, we would like that."

"This one is named Ranger, and he doesn't have a home yet. Would you like him?" asked Nate.

Chaska nodded with a smile. "Thank you," he answered.

"Of course, you could rename him with a Native American name if you want," continued Nate.

"I believe that Ranger is a strong name. We will keep it," concluded Chaska.

After tea was prepared, Elizabeth offered some cake to each of the Native Americans, along with bread and some rabbit meat left from their supper.

"Who is the hunter?" questioned Chaska as he ate.

"I am," responded Samuel. "I go everyday – sometimes for the whole day and sometimes only in the morning. I keep us supplied with meat."

"You are a good son, Samuel," commented Chaska. "Have you shot deer?"

"Last week I got a deer. I'm drying it now to store away for the winter. If we get snowed in, then we still have food," Samuel remarked with a grin.

As the Oneidas ate, the children were amazed at the sign language that was transpiring between the Native Americans. Obviously, only Chaska understood English, and he was translating for his two friends.

"Could you teach us a word?" asked Hannah finally when her curiosity got the best of her.

"What word would you like to learn?" asked Chaska.

"How do you say 'dog'?" questioned Hannah.

Chaska showed her the signal, and all of the children smiled as they signaled "dog" to each other.

"Could you move in with us for a while and teach us everything?" asked Hannah, always the one eager to learn.

Everyone laughed, but Hannah was truly serious. Elizabeth could tell by the look on her face.

When the Native Americans had finished eating, Elizabeth brought out cookies from the batch that had been made for the week, and the family shared. Conversation was limited, but the Hoyts could tell that their guests were enjoying the food.

Elizabeth thought that Nathan would be so pleased that Little Bear and his friends had come, and he'd be so proud of his children who behaved as young adults toward the Oneidas.

"It's getting very late," remarked Elizabeth. "Will you stay the night by the fire?"

"Yes," answered Chaska. "Thank you."

Elizabeth retrieved three mats from the bedrooms and laid them close to the fire for warmth. Samuel and Nate both went for more logs to put onto the fire, and the children reluctantly bid their newly-found friends good night.

By the time the children were aroused the next morning, the Native Americans were gone.

"We didn't get to say good-bye," complained Gracie. "I wanted to give Chaska a hug."

Elizabeth smiled. "Well, you will be harboring a wonderful memory of them when I make those furs into jackets for the winter," responded Elizabeth.

"Will Ranger be well taken care of?" questioned Hannah.

"Yes. Native Americans look after their animals well. I'm sure that Chaska will return one day for a visit and will bring Ranger."

* * * *

Unbeknownst to Elizabeth, Gracie – now fifteen – was thinking of joining the military as one of the ladies who washed clothes, cooked, nursed, and looked after the soldiers.

"Samuel, I'm going to join the army," Gracie whispered one day to her brother as they milked the cows. "I can't explain this feeling that I have, but it's a constant pulling at my heart strings to serve these United States in the best way that I know how."

Samuel was stunned. "What are you talking about, Gracie? I know that Pa's letters haven't told us of the nightmares of battle, but I hear of them when I'm in town. The carnage after the battles is more than most men can stand – let alone a girl. What would Ma say?"

"Ma won't know until after I'm gone. I'm going to write a letter and leave it for her."

"Just what do you think that you're going to do in the military?"

"What I'd like to do is dress like a male and be a real soldier, but I know that my small stature would give me away. My friend,

Katherine Pence, did that last year, and as far as I know, she hasn't been discovered. However, Katherine is a large young lady who could easily pass for a man when dressed in soldier's clothing."

"Yes, I heard all about women posing as men," replied Samuel. "Some have been honored and some have been disgraced. Some men were talking the other day in Lexington about Annie Corbin from Boston who wore men's clothing as she stood beside her husband at Fort Washington and took her husband's place in the middle of a battle. She was wounded, captured, and went home a disabled veteran of the war. Her good fortune was to be granted a veteran's pension."

"Really?" commented Grace.

"However, not all women are lucky, you see," continued Samuel. "There was Margaret Bailey who collected her military salary while posing as a man. However, she was eventually discovered, was discharged, fined, and put into jail for a month."

"Well, I'm planning on being a 'camp follower.' You know, one of the women who help care for the soldiers. In reality, it will be less dangerous, and, in addition, I'll be performing for my country."

Still stunned, Samuel just stared at Grace. Out of the eleven children, Ma always said that she was the most pig-headed. Samuel knew that there was no need to argue. Whenever he disagreed with Gracie, he just let it slide because he knew he couldn't win.

"When are you doing this?" he asked.

"Night after next. I have it all planned out. Don't tell anyone and don't try to stop me."

Top: Anna Strong

Bottom: Caleb Brew

CHAPTER 9

SAMUEL CULPER

Woodhull had his sight set on Caleb Brewster as a fellow spy. A bull of a man – physically huge and demanding – Brewster was intimidating even to the British. Brewster had a craving for adventure, giving up farming at the age of nineteen to become a whaler. Just as Woodhull knew the land, Brewster was well acquainted with the coves and waterways around New York City.

"You would be perfect, Caleb," confirmed Woodhull. "You'll be in the Setauket area. There will be a messenger to take the intelligence from me to you."

"Just between you and me, Abraham, I've been in correspondence with General Washington for several weeks," asserted Brewster. "I've been reporting the state of the Loyalists' warships, any important movement of the troops, and any of their naval preparations."

Woodhull was not only surprised but also impressed that Washington was trusting and using Brewster. It confirmed in his mind that Brewster was the right man for the job.

Woodhull was also interested in Austin Roe, who was married and successfully well off as a tavern owner in Setauket. Roe would be able to talk to multiple Loyalists in the tavern and hear information that would otherwise go unnoticed. There was only one problem: Would Roe be willing to sacrifice his successful position and his family if he were to be caught?

When Woodhull approached Roe one evening in his tavern, Woodhull found his friend to be remarkably interested in the prospect and eager to be of service.

"I would have very little to do differently than I already do," Roe professed. "I already listen to throngs of men as they discuss the war – both Patriots and Loyalists. I just need to listen more carefully to the Loyalists and take note of things that would be of interest to our correspondence."

As it turned out, Woodhull and Roe lived on farms that were adjacent, and they found it easy to exchange intelligence as their cattle shared a field. Roe got a metal box that could be hidden in the field, and it was there that the secret messages were placed by Woodhull to Roe. The two didn't even have to come into contact with each other.

It was now time for Tallmadge to approach Nathan Hoyt. Hoyt was called into Tallmadge's office late one afternoon.

"I have a serious matter to discuss with you, Lieutenant," Tallmadge announced. "Have a seat. General Washington has set up a secret yet well-established spy ring, and I want you to be a member. You'll carry correspondence from time to time from me to the general to dilute suspicions of my leaving my residence often.

"You see, I'm going to be living near New York City – in Setauket – and won't have any office here at the army post. If you undertake this job, you're welcome to take a room in my house in Setauket. Furthermore, understand that I must play the role now of a Loyalist in order to gain information." Tallmadge paused to ponder the situation. "That could be difficult at times, but it's what I must

do for our country. You don't need to know from whom I'm getting the correspondence as innocence is bliss in this case."

Hoyt listened intently to Tallmadge, not showing emotions
one way or the other.

After further detailed discussion about the matter, Tallmadge
asked Hoyt, "Are you willing to undertake this duty? It will
mean that you will have to swear your allegiance to the Loyalists
in order to move freely among them. I won't deny that there
could be danger at times, but I've watched you carefully for
months now. I fully believe you're capable of undertaking this
assignment. Moreover, General Washington has been more
than satisfied with your performance while fighting the enemy.
I know that you're in this war for the long haul."

Hoyt looked Tallmadge in the eye as he spoke. "Yes, I'm in
this battle to bring honor to our newly formed country – one
that I'm proud to represent. I'm happy to consent to any and
all orders concerning this prestigious work."

* * * *

Woodhull showed up unexpectedly at Tallmadge's house
one day soon after Hoyt had accepted his position in the spy
ring.

"I've heard, Benjamin, that you had some problems with
Colonel Tarleton the other day," remarked Woodhull.

"I did. You warned me of his deceitfulness, and I should have
been more attentive to your advice," replied Tallmadge. "Who
told you of my problems?"

"General Washington. Now, don't be so hard on yourself.
He's devious," stated Woodhull. "You're a good man, Benjamin,
and you take our Culper business very seriously. We all slip up.
What happened exactly?"

"Tarleton came to my house, pretending to make a social call. We sat on the porch drinking tea and chatting for about an hour. I even thought at the time that there was nothing deceptive about this man," Tallmadge said, obviously upset. "Anyway, while we were talking, my office, which is in the back of the house, was raided. A letter that Washington sent to me was in one of the drawers of my desk. It was still there when I went to my office later that afternoon, but it doesn't mean that they didn't see it."

"No, they would have taken it for evidence had they seen it," remarked Woodhull. "How do you know that they were in your office?"

"Because I always keep my desk very neat, and some of the papers were on the floor or misplaced. Plus, they stole a packet of money from Washington meant for you. Fortunately, names were not on it." Tallmadge paused for a moment, looking down at his folded hands. "I'm always very concerned for the safety of the Culper Ring and don't want any of our intelligence to be compromised. I must be careful not to leave Culper correspondence anywhere easily visible."

"Well, it was a good lesson, and we all need to be alert at all times," declared Woodhull.

"I learned, also, that Tarleton is indeed a fraud and thief. I need to be less trusting of people," concluded Tallmadge.

"I wanted to hear the story of Tarleton; however, that wasn't the real reason that I've come," continued Woodhull. "I've approached both Caleb Brewster and Austin Roe to join us as spies. They are both loyal to our cause. I'll release their names to General Washington, but I think we should refer to them by a number to keep their names secret, especially since this incident with Tarleton. What do you think?"

Tallmadge nodded.

"Have you talked with Nathan Hoyt?" asked Woodhull.

Again, Tallmadge nodded. "Yes, he's eager to be a part of this ring."

"Good. Tell me what you think of these code names. Benjamin, you'll be 721; I'll be 722 and also Samuel Culper as you previously designated. Roe will be 724; Brewster 725; Washington 711; Hoyt 726."

"Well thought out, Abraham. You've been hard at work," indicated Tallmadge. "As I recently told you, I believe that I'll also take the name of John Bolton."

Woodhull nodded. "You'll tell General Washington these details?"

"Yes, of course," replied Tallmadge.

"There's one more person, Ben. A close acquaintance of mine is Selah Strong. He was imprisoned last week by the British for his loyalty to the colonies." Woodhull stopped for a moment, his last words catching in his throat. "His wife, Anna, is a very resourceful and determined lady. She wants to help. She feels it's her duty to support what her husband stood for. He could die in the British prison for all we know." Woodhull glanced at Tallmadge before continuing. "Already she is signaling me, using her clothesline, which is clearly visible from Long Island Sound.

"A black petticoat signals the arrival of Brewster in the Sound. The number of white handkerchiefs indicates one of six coves that Brewster is in as he awaits me. Anna is adamant about helping us. If you'll accept her, she'll be 355."

Taken aback by the possibility of having a woman associated with the spy ring, Tallmadge remained silent. Finally, he spoke. "Well, Abraham, I'll suggest it to General Washington, and I'll abide by his decision."

Woodhull smiled and nodded. "I assume that Hoyt will help you get information to General Washington so that you won't be near the military. We can live our normal lives except we will be Loyalists."

"I think that everything is in place," concluded Tallmadge. "Hopefully, all of our plans will be successful in order to defeat our foe."

As Woodhull started to leave, Tallmadge called him back. "Oh, one more thing, Abraham, that Washington is going to do. The general is concerned with the fact that correspondence is written with black ink. All it would take would be one overly curious British trooper on patrol to find incriminating documents and disaster would befall the ring." Tallmadge paused. "Look how close I came with the Tarleton situation recently."

"Go on," Woodhull asserted.

"Well, the general has discovered a supply of invisible ink. The ink is normally made from onion juice, but it can also be made from other organic liquids. The point is that when you use the ink on very white paper, the letters immediately become invisible. The letters render themselves visible only when you hold candlelight to them. "

"Astounding," interjected Woodhull. "And the general has some of this ink already?"

"Not only does he have it, but also I have a vial for you. Use it sparingly as the ink is difficult to get."

Woodhull smiled. "This may help to calm my nerves a bit. I seem to be paranoid nowadays and think that everyone is trying to trip me up."

The fact of the matter was that Woodhull had been in a complete state of panic. Recently, some British officers of Colonel John Simcoe's division had unexpectedly taken up lodging in his home in Setauket. He felt sure that they suspected him of spying for the Americans.

One evening he sat in an adjacent room to the British and was writing a letter to Washington. Woodhull was nervously aware of the Redcoats in the next chamber and anxiously tried to finish his letter.

Suddenly, the door was flung open, revealing two figures. In his nervous state, Woodhull knocked over the table and all of its belongings. Woodhull expected it to be two Redcoats, but, in reality, it was his two young cousins wanting to surprise him. The entire episode only caused Woodhull's already turbulent state of mind to worsen. He became obsessed with the fear of being discovered and hanged.

However, the invisible ink would be a good solution to help relax Woodhull's anxious state.

In order for the invisible ink to work well, it was important that the members of the ring write on new, white paper from that point on, despite the added expense and the difficulty of acquiring it. They needed the whitest paper available.

At some point, they began to realize the scarcity of the ink. The Culpers – as they were now called – often found themselves grievously short of the ink, and Washington openly told Tallmadge to preserve the precious drops. Woodhull tended to hoard it for fear of not having any.

It was during this time that the British retrieved a brief letter written in black ink by Tallmadge because he had run out of invisible ink. Fortunately, Tallmadge had signed the letter "John Bolton." However, the British now knew that a ring existed between New York City and across Connecticut. Immediately, the Culpers developed a code so that intelligence couldn't be read.

The number 1 would represent either the letter C or R. Number 2 would represent D or S. Number 3 would represent E or T, and so on. In addition, the Culpers made codes for words used frequently – New York City, 720; Setauket, 729; England, 745; George Washington, 711; peace, 470; Tory, 639; tyranny, 646. This coded message **k.ni.219.72.592.in.727.473** would mean: k=5, ni=74, 219= gun, 72=British, 592= ship, in=in, 727=New York, 473=port. Thus, the message would read: **5 74-gun British ships in New York port.**

From that point on, all the letters would be coded to secure secrecy.

Even though Nathan in his letters home would have to keep being part of the spy ring a secret from Elizabeth, he felt compelled to let her know that his circumstances had changed. He would be sure to do that as soon as he could get a letter written and mailed to her.

CHAPTER 10

LETTER FROM NATHAN AND
AT HOME IN LEXINGTON

Dearest Elizabeth

I have had a change in my station in the army. I cannot relay to you what I am doing, but it is different than fighting on the battlefields. It is a position that only a few people know about, and I am proud to be a part of this placement – and, may I say, promotion. I am still in danger as are all of us in the army, but it is a different kind of hazard and risk. I wish that I could tell you more, but you must be sure that God is watching over me every minute of my life here.

For the most part, I'll not be fighting in battles now. I'm very glad of that because I didn't realize how debilitating battles could be. To experience the shooting of cannons and musketry, to see the fire and smoke, to hear the whistling of a rifle shot is all horrible. I have hated seeing someone shot or taken prisoner. It's not something that any man wants to see. The fighting causes anxiety, fatigue, and hardships, and I'm glad that I won't be directly involved now.

I find that many of the soldiers are worried about their families during this third year of the war. We all are concerned that our wives have been left to run everything at home and that our children are growing up without fathers.

In addition, we know that the currency in America is nearly worthless. We understand that it's the same in England. We often question how we thought that we could beat the biggest and best army in the world. Thus, any victories that we achieve help to brighten our decision to have gone to war in the first place.

Well, I don't want to dwell on heartaches and battles. I would rather tell you about an incident that occurred a few days ago, and I hope that I helped in the outcome.

An Irishman belonging to our infantry saw a wounded man belonging to the enemy lying on the roadside. He took pity on him as the Redcoat was in danger of being trod upon by horses. O'Reilly, the Irishman, shouldered the Redcoat and attempted to carry him to safety. He happened to jostle the poor fellow more than necessary, and the Redcoat cried out, "Good Rebel, don't hurt a poor Hessian." O'Reilly responded, "Who do you call a Rebel, you scoundrel?" With that he threw the Redcoat off his shoulder and walked off.

I saw it all happening and went to help the enemy soldier off the road and into the woods where I had to leave him. I silently prayed that the Redcoats would find him and give him assistance. When I returned to the area later that night, the soldier was gone, and I have to believe that he had been found by his men.

Often, we feel as if we have little to smile about in the military ranks; however, something happened several weeks ago that brought smiles to all of us. It happened to one of my friends, Thomas Franklin, who was fighting in the battles and normally looking for food during the day. Several of the soldiers and he stopped at a small farmhouse, and a mother and her child came out.

The child was about four years old, and they were told she had been cross and crying all day. The mother said that she had been threatening the child that she was going to give her to the Yankees. Thomas spoke up saying, "We are Yankees." The woman looked shocked and retorted, "You are Yankees? I thought that you were Pennsylvanians. You look very normal to me." Thomas said that they all let out a howl. I had to laugh at it as well.

Something else that I want to tell you about. We experienced a very strange situation some weeks back. I don't know if you had a "dark day" on May 19 or not. I heard it wasn't as bad in Massachusetts as in some of the other colonies in New England. It became so dark in Pennsylvania where we were that day that the chickens went to their roosts and the whip-poor-wills sang their nighttime serenade. In addition, people had to light candles during the day in order to carry on business as usual. That night, it was just as uncommonly dark as the day was. It was such a strange day and night, and one like I've never experienced before.

I believe everyone wishes there would be a cessation of duty from the army with a chance to go home for a month. Spending time with family and friends would help everyone's morale. Of course, this is an impossibility, but men continue to talk of it, especially those who are so poorly dressed and hungry.

I must say that I enjoy my time discussing matters and just chatting with Lafayette and Hamilton. They are both incredible soldiers as well as perfect gentlemen. It helps to take my mind off of fighting when we have evening chats, sometimes around a fire.

My love to all of you. I stretch out my arms and send you hugs.

Your loving husband,
Nathan

* * * *

By now, Elizabeth had gotten used to the fact that Grace had left for the military. Alone in bed, she cried, but she wouldn't allow the children to see this. She needed to stay strong for them. Besides, she had little time to dwell on her loss.

Patsy arrived early one morning with Jewel at her heels. She was obviously in a state of panic, and Elizabeth pulled her indoors quickly.

"Patsy? What's wrong?"

"My dad's very sick. The doctor came last night, and he believes it is diphtheria." By then, Patsy was sobbing. "My ma wants to know if I can stay here so that I don't get sick."

Elizabeth took Patsy in her arms. "Of course, Patsy. You're more than welcome. You already know that, darling."

"I don't want to leave my ma, though."

Patsy tried very hard to control her emotions, but she was failing.

"Your ma knows best," Elizabeth stated. "Now, come on and sit at the table. I'll get tea for you. Have you slept at all?"

"No. I'm fine, though."

"Let me get you a bite to eat, and then we'll get you to bed for a bit. The girls will be happy to have another sister."

The truth was, having Patsy would help to make up for Grace's absence. Elizabeth couldn't replace Gracie, but she could help fill the empty spot with Patsy.

Elizabeth tried to be complaisant in front of Patsy, but she silently said a prayer for Sean as well as Violet. Diphtheria was not a disease to take lightly.

Jewel was already scratching at the girls' bedroom door to see the other dogs as well as the children. All the puppies had been given away to other people in Lexington. With two dogs already at the Hoyt residence, Elizabeth had said "no" to keeping any of the babies.

"There will be more puppies in the future," Elizabeth had said. "Once this war is over...."

* * * *

The teacher discussed the war with the children each day at school in order to educate them on the important events since many of their fathers were in battle. Americans were trying to establish their freedom, and it was obviously a difficult task.

One afternoon, Hannah and Nate came home discussing the Marquis de Lafayette.

"Yes, Hannah, he is from France and has been in this country for a while," stated Nate.

"What are you talking about?" questioned Elizabeth, hearing Lafayette's name mentioned.

"Our teacher was telling of Lafayette's duties in our army,

and, of course, we perked up because Pa has mentioned him in his correspondence."

Elizabeth was interested. "What did you learn?"

"Mrs. Haley, our teacher, said that General Washington and the Marquis de Lafayette have formed a bond and that the General trusts Lafayette for important missions. He has even asked the marquis to help secure his troops and disrupt British communication in Philadelphia and New York City."

"How does she know this?" Elizabeth asked.

"Her husband also works closely with Washington as an aide to take messages to troops in battle," responded Nate.

"He must be an essential man in General Washington's network," concluded Elizabeth.

"There's more, Ma," inserted Hannah. "To achieve his goal, Lafayette has been asked to find trusty and intelligent spies to communicate to him whatever has been happening in New York City and Philadelphia."

"Because of Pa's friendship with Lafayette, could he possibly be helping him as a spy? I mean, he says his job cannot be discussed, and Pa is trusty and intelligent." Nate paused. "What do you think, Ma?"

"Of course, anything is possible, son, but we know nothing for sure. Being a spy seems extremely treacherous, and your father hasn't made it seem that his job is more dangerous than the battlefield."

"No, but he wrote that he's still in danger but of a different kind. Spying would call for a different kind of danger, don't you think?" questioned Nate.

"Well, we have no way of knowing his current job, so we will have to wait until he returns home to learn details. Now, there are chores awaiting all of you."

* * * *

At the evening meal, Elizabeth noticed that all of the children were involved in the conversation except for Samuel. With downcast eyes, he picked at his food. Patsy was now a participant with Hannah and Nate in the conversation about the Marquis de Lafayette, but Samuel remained silent. After supper, Elizabeth put the children in charge of cleaning up and motioned Samuel to go outside with her.

"Samuel, is something bothering you?"

"No, not really. Well, yes, I guess that there is something that I need to discuss with you, but I don't know how to begin."

"Your pa always says to 'blurt it out,' so I say that *that* is the best thing to do. Perhaps, I can help," Elizabeth speculated.

"Ma, you know that Magdalena O'Brien and I have been close friends this past year." He paused, awaiting an answer.

"Yes, she has been here on many occasions for supper, and you go to her house often. Are you in love with her, son?"

Once more, Samuel's eyes were downcast while he fidgeted with his sleeve.

"Ma, I'm seventeen now, and, yes, I'm in love with Magdalena. More importantly, though, I want to get married."

Hardly expecting that to come out of her son's mouth, she simply gaped at him for a moment.

Elizabeth tried to keep her voice steady. "You are young yet, son."

"You and Pa were married when you were sixteen. Now more than ever with the war ongoing, we do not know what our futures bring. I may perhaps enlist at some time, and then I want to know that I have a wife waiting for me."

These were the thoughts of a young, foolish person. Having a wife awaiting her spouse's return made it even more difficult for both people.

"It's very hard to leave behind not only a wife but perhaps also a child, Samuel. Are you really sure that this is what you want? It seems so sudden."

"It's not sudden," Samuel stated. "Magdalena and I have discussed it at length for six months now, and it's what we both want. We don't know what is forthcoming, but we know that we want our futures intertwined. That can only mean marriage, Ma." Samuel paused a moment. "I did not want to say anything to Magdalena's parents until I talked with you."

"Can't your lives be intertwined without being married? Aren't your lives linked – interwoven – now without marriage?" Elizabeth asked.

"We want to be 'one,' Ma."

Elizabeth stopped, absorbing what Samuel really wanted. It was true that to be 'one,' marriage was eminent. Elizabeth was slowly coming around to the thoughts that Samuel had expressed.

"Your father is not here, but if he were, I believe that he and I together would commend you for your choice of a young lady. She is polite, responsible, trustworthy, and religious – all of the things that you want in a wife and mother."

Elizabeth took Samuel's hand in hers. "Go to her parents, son, and ask permission."

Samuel's smile and shining eyes told it all. He kissed his mother and left on his horse.

Elizabeth sat with her hands folded for a long time. Wishing that Nathan were there would not make things any better, but if a wedding were to take place, she wished for her husband's presence.

CHAPTER 11

THE SPIES GROW

General Washington had found a true friend and comrade in Marquis de Lafayette, whose loyalty to the newly formed United States of America was credible as well as impressive. Lafayette took every opportunity to secure Washington's camp and endeavored to obtain intelligence from any British communication that passed his way. The latter finally pushed Lafayette to employ spies to help him. Thus, he looked to his friend, Nathan Hoyt.

Hoyt had taken the offer made by Tallmadge to stay in a room in his house in Setauket so that Hoyt could make frequent visits – normally in disguise – to Washington's Camp.

"It's an honor to have you in America," Hoyt said one day to Lafayette. "I heard from General Washington himself that you won him over after the Battle of Brandywine during your four weeks of convalescence with your leg injury. The general heard nothing but good comments about you from the surgeons and nurses at the care facility," declared Hoyt. "Above all, you became an intermediary between the French and the Americans."

Lafayette bowed his head in humility. "Thank you, Lieutenant. It's very kind of you to offer such endearing compliments."

"They're true. After your injury healed and you rejoined our army in October, your ardor and goodwill continued to make an impression on the general, at which time he named you commander of a division. With someone so young as you, that just doesn't happen normally," Hoyt proclaimed.

"Thank you again for your kind words. I am humbled to be of service to this great country. "

Lafayette paused a moment to retrieve a letter from his desk. "However, Lieutenant, I must ask a military favor of you now," Lafayette confessed. "General Washington has written a request of me that I'd like to read to you. Do you mind?"

"Oh, please, read it," responded Hoyt.

"I'll refrain from reading the entire letter but rather read just the part that is the petition of which I speak: 'Above all, we must endeavor to provide security to this camp and to disrupt British communications with their spies, which we know are prevalent in Philadelphia and New York City. We need to obstruct the incursions of the enemy parties and obtain intelligence of their motions and designs. To achieve this goal, Marquis, I need for you to procure trusty and intelligent spies, who will advise you faithfully of whatever may be passing in the city.'"

Lafayette hesitated, looking at Hoyt. "General Washington has confidence in me, and I must not fail him."

"Of course," Hoyt answered.

"I'm asking if you would be willing to help?" the marquis questioned.

"You're asking me to be a spy for you?"

Lafayette nodded. "I am, Lieutenant."

"Yes, of course, I will help. However, you need to understand that I won't be your most available person as I'm quite busy with Washington's work in the city. I have little spare time, but when I'm free, I'll be honored to assist you. Please, just let me know."

* * * *

By now, it was known that spies were everywhere, both Loyalists to Britain as well as Patriots to the Americans. Woodhull's unwanted British troops had finally moved out of his house, but Woodhull continually kept his eye on Simcoe, whom he had learned to suspect of just about everything. Simcoe was indeed a devious man. However, Woodhull was now in a state of anxiety because of several other circumstances that had happened recently.

First, Woodhull had recently been invited to a dinner given in honor of several commanders in the British army. He had felt uncomfortable being among only Redcoats, all chatting and discussing the war. It was an excellent way to pick up intelligence needed by the spy ring, but it had left Woodhull anxious.

On top of that, Woodhull had sat across from General Henry Clinton, who was continually eyeing Woodhull. Whenever Woodhull looked up, Clinton was watching him, making Woodhull very uncomfortable. It didn't help when Clinton had started asking him questions. As soon as it was possible, Woodhull had excused himself and made for home. His biggest worry was that he was suspected of spying. He knew that he had become paranoid as of late, but it was increasingly difficult for Woodhull to calm his nerves.

Secondly, several weeks later, the ultimate happened. Colonel Simcoe, the officer who had stayed at Woodhull's house with British troops, showed up at Woodhull's home in Setauket to arrest Woodhull on suspicion of espionage.

Simcoe and his soldiers had surrounded Woodhull's home with their muskets poised, but, fortunately, Woodhull was in New York City at his sister's house. Simcoe was sure that Woodhull would learn of their visit and dispose of any incriminating evidence that he might have. Of greatest misfortune, the British had bludgeoned Woodhull's elderly father, leaving him crumpled on the ground.

With these two situations weighing on Woodhull's mind both day and night, he was left in utter despair. When he had an opportunity, Woodhull called upon Tallmadge, begging for some help. Woodhull reported to Tallmadge that he believed that going into New York City so often was making him look suspicious. Tallmadge could understand the situation and agreed with Woodhull. The first chance that he got, Tallmadge recounted the fact to Washington, who consented to having someone help relieve a bit of the pressure off Woodhull. Washington had a man in mind and relayed the name of the person to Woodhull.

It was thought that men wanted to become a spy for bragging rights later on in life or for the financial security that it rendered for the present time. Mild-mannered, bookwormish, Robert Townsend fit into neither of these categories. He was a peaceful, quiet man with independent ways and mindset. He was the type of man that the general wanted in his spy ring in New York City center.

Townsend had stayed out of the war until viewing the present calamity at his boyhood home, called Raynham Hall, the most exquisite house in Oyster Bay.

On a recent visit home, Townsend had seen firsthand behavior from the British that would turn many Loyalists into Patriots. Townsend had found that his father had been physically forced by Colonel John Simcoe to house British troops, just as he had done to Woodhull previously. The Redcoats forcibly set up headquarters in the main part of the house, and the family was relocated into a few back rooms.

With all of the extra work and stresses of having Loyalists living with him, Townsend's father bore a very defeated, worn appearance. In the weeks following his visit home, Townsend was haunted and outraged by what he had seen, and when Woodhull approached him with a proposal to become a spy, Townsend readily agreed with the plan. He, as well as Woodhull, hated Simcoe.

Townsend ran a shop close to the harbor of New York City and was privy to many conversations of both Americans and British. Woodhull realized that Townsend's position in New York City gave him access to potentially valuable information for the ring.

"This will be perfect, Robert, because you will have a far greater chance of getting intelligence since you are closer to the center of New York City than any of the other spies, and you can mix with numerous British and public figures," asserted Woodhull. "In addition, you can pay particular attention to the movements of the Loyalists by land and water in and about the city.

"I, also, believe that you will be able to find out how well the British are provisioned and, also, what the morale and health of the British soldiers are." Woodhull paused for a moment to consider his next thought. "In the end, Robert, you will be able to gather data and documents better than anyone else in the ring and get the information to me by way of a messenger."

Townsend sat with his hands clasped, obviously processing the information. Finally, he looked up at Woodhull, giving him a nod.

"I have already thought this all through, Robert, and I would give you the name of Samuel Culper, Jr. I'd readjust my name to Samuel Culper, Sr.," Woodhull announced. "And your code number would be 723."

Townsend sat, again thinking of the facts and data being thrown at him. "A double life would certainly disrupt whatever calm I now have, and I'd have to insist that no one other than you know about this," Townsend attested.

"Yes. I would say nothing, not even to General Washington himself; however, he came up with your name," confirmed Woodhull.

Townsend was shocked. "How does he know anything about me?"

"I don't ask questions of the general when he gives me an order," replied Woodhull.

Woodhull held his hand out for Townsend to shake.

Townsend extended his hand. A serious agreement had been comprised, and Townsend knew that he now could demonstrate his steadfast allegiance to his country. Immediately, he took part in the charade and swore his allegiance to the Crown.

As it came to be, Townsend's detailed reports on naval activities became far more precise than any Woodhull had been able to provide. Townsend even found a way of making his messages harder to find by the Redcoats. He would buy a set of new sheets of paper, write his message in invisible ink on one of the sheets, and insert it at a prearranged place in the papers.

Townsend also wrote his messages on the blank pages of pamphlets and books or between the lines of already written letters. His expertise was helpful and also valuable in getting intelligence to other members of the ring.

Besides all of this, Washington wanted Townsend to find out how many soldiers were in New York City and where they were stationed. Townsend was to try to find out how many small forts there were and how many cannons were ready for battle. Washington also hoped that Townsend could establish how well the Redcoats were provisioned and what their morale and health were like. It was an intricate and massive assignment, but Townsend did his job well, and, at all times, Washington was pleased and often surprised at the details and complexity of the intelligence.

In addition to all of this, Townsend was adamant about finding a way to move more freely throughout the city unnoticed. He discovered a coffee house and print shop run by James Rivington, an English expatriate.

Townsend applied for a job with Rivington's newspaper so he could occasionally write a column of local interest. It turned out to be a brilliant idea because now Townsend had the perfect excuse to migrate more freely about the city, to ask questions, and to trace various movements of the British troops.

Despite Rivington's allegiance to the Loyalists, he and Townsend developed a bond of friendship during Townsend's time spent at Rivington's coffee house and while writing for the newspaper. Townsend openly shared his feelings about the British to Rivington, who was surprisingly impressed with the Patriots' inclinations.

Ironically in the fall of 1778, Rivington threw in his lot with the Patriots and worked with Townsend to gather information about the British and convey it to General Washington himself. Rivington proved a valuable asset to Townsend and the Culpers.

Oh, how Nathan wished he could write home about the spy ring and the brave men who risked their lives to give General Washington the information he so sorely needed. Knowing that he must remain silent, not a word was written in his homebound letters.

CHAPTER 12

LETTER FROM NATHAN AND AT HOME IN LEXINGTON

Dearest Elizabeth,

My work continues, and I wish that I could tell you about it. Just know that I am as safe as possible in this ungodly world that we live in. Even some of the Redcoats find refuge with us, becoming turncoats when they cannot stand the dreadful rules of the Redcoat militia. Apparently, they are living in an uncivilized world as well.

I will tell you that my friendship with the Marquis de Lafayette is continuing. Last night, he told me of the battle that he experienced some months ago at Barren Hill, a few miles from Philadelphia.

He said that while his troop waited to see the Redcoats, a company of about a hundred Native Americans joined them. There was a hill close to them on which an old church was built. It was nearly devastated, and the Native Americans amused themselves by shooting their arrows at the dilapidated structure. The marquis said that one of the arrows hit a cluster of bats – nearly a bushel of them hanging under one of the eaves. Immediately, the Native Americans took sport in trying to catch the bats. He said that he knew not how many bats, but he had never seen so many before nor since – indeed, in his whole life put together. We had a great laugh over it, and I can still smile when I think of the scene that the marquis had experienced.

As I was going to the post of General Washington last week, I saw an unusual sight. At least I had not seen it before. There was a broad ring of men standing in a circle watching something of a spectacle. Two Irishmen – I was told that they were Irish because I did not know the men – were stripped to the buff and were prepared to fight. It was not fighting as you would imagine, but rather it was boxing. I was told that it was the second bout, and both men were bloody as butchers. I was not able to stay and watch as I had a message to deliver to the general, but it was a sight to see.

I attempt to continually tell you of tidbits of stories that help lighten my day. The battles are bloody and horrendous, but, fortunately, I am not in any of them. I definitely hear about them from my fellow soldiers.

I heard an interesting story about Admiral Charles d'Estaing – of the French navy – the other day. It was not really strictly about d'Estaing but rather his French navy troops who have been helping us. It was after d'Estaing left General John Sullivan in Rhode Island, where they had together been fighting the British, and sailed with his troops to Boston.

Once in Boston, the French set up a bakery on the shore to supply their ships. Since flour had vanished from the Boston markets, a crowd of local people tried to buy French bread. The baker spoke no English, and the Bostonians spoke no French. An argument and then a riot ensued, and a young French soldier by the name of Chevalier de Saint-Sauveur was killed.

With diminutive tact, the episode was brushed aside and even blamed on the British, who had been absent during the argument. But in another way, the incident made history: Saint-Sauveur's funeral was conducted by a Franciscan priest in a secret ceremony, and it was the very first Roman Catholic Mass ever said in Boston, an interesting fact of history undertaken during the American Revolution.

I must close, my darling. I am sending to you all of my love.

Your loving husband,
Nathan

* * * *

It was mid-December, and Samuel and Magdalena had already been married six months.

"I'd love to build an added room to the rear of my parents' house just for us. It would give us peace and privacy. What do you think, Magdalena?"

Magdalena thought for a moment. "Well, you know, Samuel, there is the spare bedroom that we've been staying in. It's perfectly fine, and we have plenty of privacy. I think that I'd rather just continue on as we have been doing. Then, when this war is over, we can think about building our own house nearby. What do you think?"

"Are you fine with this decision?" questioned Samuel.

"Yes, of course. I get along great with your sisters and Patsy. I totally feel like one of the family," replied Magdalena with a smile.

"All right then. It's settled. Once the war is over, we'll look into building our own place," declared Samuel, returning Magdalena's smile.

With the Christmas season quickly approaching, the children took advantage of the evenings to start making gifts and covertly hiding them in their mattresses. With little money to spare, inexpensive, simple presents were created.

The girls had unraveled an old sweater of Hannah's and were knitting socks for their two brothers and a potholder for their mother. The boys had melted an old pewter tool and were making spoons for their mother and the three girls.

With joy of the season upon them, the Hoyts attempted to bring some happiness to Patsy and help her cope with the first Christmas without her parents. Knowing it would be a difficult time for her, the girls made a special attempt to include her in every single project that they undertook. Seeing Patsy smile brought exceptional joy to each girl.

Now with Magdalena a part of the family, Patsy had decided to take on the last name of "Hoyt" as well, so as to truly be one of the brood. Even more exciting, everyone in the household called Elizabeth "Ma," and she could not have been happier.

A day before Christmas Eve, the children went into the woods to choose a small evergreen to decorate. They made simple ornaments and assembled paper chains to decorate the tree. Patsy had a star brought from Ireland to top the small fir. Last of all, candles were strategically placed so as not to cause a fire.

Christmas Eve arrived with a light snow, and the family made their way to church in the middle of Lexington.

"Christmas Eve is one of my favorite evenings of the year," declared Nate.

"Mine, too," chimed in Hannah. "I especially love it when there is a little snow like tonight."

The congregation arrived at the church from all sides of the city, candles in hand illuminating the way. It created an aurora of light from all directions.

It was midnight as the Hoyts made their way home through the streets and then through the darkened woods. As they appeared in the clearing, their house shown with candles burning and smoke spiraling from the chimney.

"We left no candles burning!" exclaimed Elizabeth with astonishment. "And there was no fire in the fireplace!"

"Could it be Pa?" asked Hannah, enthusiastically.

"We can't know that for sure," replied Elizabeth. "Samuel, go to the shed quietly and retrieve an axe. It is our only weapon available. The rifles are in the house."

It was a long ten minutes until Samuel returned, axe in hand.

"Children, wait here while Samuel and I find out what's happening."

With the curtains closed, there was no way to see into the house, and no noise was heard.

"Let me knock on the door, Samuel. You stand back out of sight in case you need to attack."

With a light tap on the door, Elizabeth waited.

"Who's there?" came a voice.

"Elizabeth Hoyt. Who are you?"

The door swung opened to reveal a Redcoat.

"Is this your house?"

Elizabeth nodded.

"Are you alone?"

"No, my family is with me. Why are you here?"

"I have an injured soldier. We needed cover, and your house was the first one we came upon. Stay quiet, and no one will be hurt. No weapons so if you have any, leave them outside. I will put our rifles outside the door as well," stated the soldier. "We mean no harm to any of you."

"Samuel, put the axe down," remarked Elizabeth as she signaled for the children.

An injured Redcoat was on the floor next to the fireplace, blood seeping from his shoulder. A blanket retrieved from the Redcoat's knapsack had absorbed a great deal of blood. A sleeve from a shirt was acting as a tourniquet with little success.

"He needs a doctor," Elizabeth noted.

"No, we will be taken prisoner. Do you know anything to help him?" the soldier asked.

"Not really," replied Elizabeth.

"I can help," Patsy interrupted. "My mother was a nurse, and I learned from her. I need hot water, disinfectant, and a knife, please, Ma."

Elizabeth smiled at the familiarity of the language and nodded.

It was a long night as Patsy removed a bullet and used sewing equipment to close the wound. Elizabeth took a pillowcase to shred into strips for bandages.

Sometime during the operation when the injured Redcoat – Private Arnold Hoff – seemed stable, the uninjured soldier went outside for a breath of air and was smoking a cigarette, gazing at the stars when Samuel opened the door.

Samuel had seen the soldier retreat to the outdoors and wanted to make sure that he wasn't getting his rifle or doing anything that would harm the family.

"My name is Samuel Hoyt," Samuel offered as he stepped onto the porch.

"I am Lieutenant Henry Austin. I arrived here in the colonies from London a few months ago. Never in my younger days did I ever think that I would be fighting in a war in the British colonies."

There was silence as the lieutenant continued to look at the stars.

"I bet that you don't know what the brightest star is in the sky," Austin commented, pointing to a sparkling constellation overhead.

"That's Sirius," replied Samuel.

Lieutenant Austin looked at Samuel somewhat impressed. "Yes, son, you are correct."

"Did you know, too, that it's made up of two stars, actually?" asserted Samuel.

"Why, yes, that's true," replied the lieutenant. "You are quite well informed."

"I'm interested in the universe – galaxies and all." Samuel paused, grateful that the lieutenant was simply getting a breath of air and smoking a cigarette.

"Well, I need to get back inside and see if I can be of any help. Excuse me, Lieutenant," inserted Samuel.

It was near dawn when the surgery was completed. The children had fallen asleep in the living area, and Elizabeth did not want to move them.

Patsy lay near the fire, close to the injured soldier. Elizabeth and Samuel each took a chair and quickly dozed.

By mid-morning, the family had arisen, and Elizabeth suggested that she and the girls make a Christmas dinner. Samuel and Nate retrieved potatoes and corn from the cellar along with deer meat that had been hung and dried. Lieutenant Austin produced bread and apples to contribute to the dinner.

By early afternoon, everyone, including Private Hoff, was seated at the table.

"Shall we say a prayer of thanksgiving?" suggested Elizabeth.

"May I?" asked Patsy.

Elizabeth nodded and smiled.

"Thank you, Lord, for this most memorable Christmas Day. Last night, the holiest of nights, we were given a task straight from you, Lord. We were asked to help the enemy. It was something you would have done while you walked the earth, and we complied with the request. With my limited knowledge, you helped me, making this a miraculous Christmas – one we will all remember."

Patsy's voice faltered with a quiet sob, and Elizabeth continued. "Thank you, God, for the birth of your Son. It has been a joyous Christmas Day. In your name, Amen."

* * * *

Unbeknownst to Nathan, Gracie was but twenty miles from the route that he took to deliver messages to General Washington.

Gracie found that the work was difficult, but she was a faithful assistant wherever needed, and she felt a sense of accomplishment on a daily basis. She worked longer hours than she had at home, and she fell onto the straw mattress feeling a sense of joy for having helped her country.

Lieutenant John Darr, who was in charge of the soldiers and reported directly to General Washington, called Grace into his hut one bitterly cold morning. The soldiers had had only good things to report about Grace – her responsiveness and her attentiveness to all duties – and the lieutenant needed a good woman for a delicate assignment. A spy in a British camp.

"You'll enter the British camp and ask to be a helper with food and laundry," Darr remarked.

"A 'camp follower,'" interrupted Gracie.

Darr nodded. "Yes, exactly. It'll take at least a month for you to build allegiance with the Redcoats, but in time, you'll have their trust and will be able to listen to conversations.

"With winter here, there'll be no battles for several months, so by March, you'll slip away and return here. It's a dangerous assignment only if you can't keep up your façade." Lieutenant Darr paused, looking directly into Grace's eyes. "Could you do this?"

"I can," responded Grace with determination. It was an assignment which she knew God had allocated to her.

"The Escape of Sergeant Champe" (Currier and Ives)

CHAPTER 13

MORE SPY ACTIVITY: JOHN CHAMPE AND BENEDICT ARNOLD

I t was about this time in 1779 that Major General Benjamin Lincoln, who was leading the American Army in Charleston, South Carolina, had to completely surrender to the British. The American prisoners were crowded onto British prison ships.

Previously, the British had sent prisoners to New York, where thirteen separate penitentiaries had been established to house the prisoners of war. However, now, the British had resolved the matter by converting obsolete naval vessels into prison ships.

The prisoners were faced with some of the most disastrous situations imaginable. Their rations were inadequate in quantity and nutrition, and often the food was spoiled or swarming with maggots or worms. In addition, clothing and bedding were totally inadequate.

The wardens on the vessels were said to be barbarous. Some allegedly punished the prisoners with beatings, inadequate water in hot weather, and cells that were dark and damp. With little sunshine and fresh air, the vessels held an unspeakable stench of illness and human waste. To be sure, the conditions were abominable and definitely contributed to the phrase heard throughout the South by 1780: "These are the times that tried men's souls."

There was one special miracle, though, that did happen on the field, which was a grassy meadow, after the Battle of Charleston. The fighting had been grueling before the Redcoats declared victory, and there was ample devastation. Since the battlefield had been a meadow, there had been cows grazing before the fighting started. Blood gathered around the cattle that had been killed, and small areas of meat from the cows had been sliced off. Obviously, some steaks for the Redcoats had been pilfered.

Amidst the dead cows were also Patriots lying in their own blood. They were, of course, left behind when the captured soldiers were taken aboard the ship. Nathan's friend, Jonas Browning, had been among the soldiers who had been left for dead. Months later, he revealed the incident to Nathan.

"I was lying in the field next to several of my friends who also had been shot and were dead," stated Jonas. "I was in great pain because a bullet had passed through what I believe to have been my lung and blood was spilling out of my mouth. I knew that I was near death."

"Oh, Jonas," Nathan declared. "Yet here you are!"

"Yes, well, I was praying to our Maker and hoped that my life would end soon, and I could join the Lord when a Patriot commander appeared at my side."

"'Peace be with you, Jonas,'" he said. His voice was comforting yet strong, and I immediately questioned how he could possibly be standing there when all of our soldiers were either dead or had been taken prisoner. As the commander continued to talk – about what, I don't remember – my pain started to lessen, and I felt the greatest peace that I've ever felt in my life. This continued on for I judge maybe fifteen minutes. Soon, I felt no pain at all.

By then, I also felt well enough to stand, and he took my hand and helped me up. I looked around the field to make sure that there were no Redcoats, and I started to thank the soldier, but he was gone." Jonas paused, wiping a tear that had slipped from his eye.

"He was an angel, Nathan. There is no other explanation. I had no pain, and I was healed. I snuck into the woods and stayed there through the night. In the morning, a platoon of Patriots appeared to bury the dead and found me. I couldn't tell them what had happened because they wouldn't have believed me. They would have thought that I'd had hallucinations."

"Jonas, it was a miracle. There's no other explanation," responded Nathan.

"Yes, a miracle. The moments that I spent with that 'angel' will stay with me forever. The healing, the peace, the love – it was as if I were in the presence of our Maker. I don't imagine that I'll ever feel those feelings again until I arrive in Heaven."

* * * *

The British had always been known to be excellent counterfeiters, and Benjamin Tallmadge knew it. It became a great way to devalue the Patriots' money if counterfeit money were manufactured. Tallmadge became aware of a counterfeiting plot in New York City.

As the American economy began to take a downward spiral, Tallmadge began to investigate a group of Loyalists on board ships in the harbor of New York City. There seemed to be a siege of activities transpiring in the harbor, and Tallmadge had suspected for some time that they were up to no good. Finally, he surmised it could be counterfeiting since there was a constant flow of businessmen, bankers whom he knew from past experience on and off the ship.

Tallmadge reported his suspicions to Washington who then ordered a special paper of extremely high quality to be used in the American money being minted in Philadelphia. Even that didn't work because a possible double agent procured the information about the paper, and soon money was coming from New York City with the same excellent quality, and it was counterfeit.

Attempts to destroy the war effort through manufacturing counterfeit bills was not new, but America's economy was in a dire state. Tallmadge continued to watch the goings-on of the men on and off the ship. Finally, he decided to board the ship himself under the guise of being a Philadelphia banker. It didn't take too many weeks for Tallmadge to unveil the plot and report to Washington of his findings.

Through the discovery of the counterfeit bills, the Americans had unmasked the entire counterfeiting plot of the enemy and stopped the activities before they reached catastrophic proportions. The British had no way of knowing for sure how the Americans knew of their secrets, so the Culpers were still secure. Tallmadge had again shown his true colors as a spy, and Washington made a special effort to congratulate him.

* * * *

In the late summer of 1780, General Henry Clinton was poised to spring a trap on the Patriots. Clinton's goal was to capture West Point, a key American stronghold on the Hudson River that allowed Washington to move his men, supplies, and arms from Massachusetts and Connecticut to other colonies. General Benedict Arnold was West Point's commander.

Marquis de Lafayette had heard the entire story of Benedict Arnold and opted to share it with Hoyt one night as they sat outside their hut in an attempt to stay cool.

"You know, Arnold's military laurels to the Patriots were unsurpassed. He fought valiantly at Fort Ticonderoga and played a decisive role at Saratoga," began Lafayette. "However, he was resentful that he was continually passed over for promotion, and he thought he was not given honors due him for his brave service. When Arnold was recuperating in Philadelphia after a leg injury, he grew increasingly uncomfortable with our French alliance and more complacent with the Loyalists' views."

"How do you know this?" questioned Hoyt.

"Because I was with him while he was recovering in Philadelphia, and I heard all of his complaints about the Patriots. Fearing that he was possibly going to be a turncoat, I mentioned it to General Washington, but there was no evidence yet, so nothing was done," declared Lafayette.

"Anyway, hindsight is better than foresight, and I believe that because of this change of heart, Arnold was determined to get sketches of West Point and maps of its artillery positions to the British at White Plains, New York. He chose John Andre, a good friend of his, to be the messenger. Unbeknownst to us at that time, Andre was a Loyalist, posing as a Patriot," stated Lafayette.

"Andre had the incriminating plans of West Point hidden in his stocking. When he came into contact with Patriots, they found the telltale documents and detained him. The jig was up, and it was just a matter of time before Andre was arrested. Like our Patriot Nathan Hale, Loyalist John Andre had been caught red-handed in the act of espionage and could not escape. Eventually, he was hanged," concluded Lafayette.

"I was there in camp that day when the Patriots brought Andre in for examination and execution, but I couldn't stay to watch as I was on assignment," admitted Hoyt. "I have to say that I, too, thought about Nathan Hale and what he must have gone through before his hanging. In my opinion, Andre paid his life for Benedict Arnold's treason." Hoyt paused. "However, Andre was a Loyalist posing as a Patriot, so he did get his due punishment in the end."

Meanwhile, word got out to the Patriots of Arnold becoming a traitor, and the Culpers worried that he possibly knew names of the ring.

Tallmadge made a special trip to visit Washington. "General, with Arnold becoming a turncoat, the Culpers are a bit worried what information he might have about us."

"Understandable," remarked Washington.

"They wanted me to relay to you that they are too apprehensive of danger to give their immediate attention to the intelligence of the ring," proclaimed Tallmadge.

"I understand that as well. Perhaps, just lie low for a bit until we can learn more about the information that Arnold has. If Arnold has ample evidence of the ring, I will make a plan for his removal." Washington paused. "Not death to start with but rather imprisonment so we can interrogate him."

"All right, General. We'll decrease correspondence for a few weeks if that is agreeable with you."

Washington nodded.

Eventually the tumult subsided, and for a while matters returned to normal for the spy ring.

However, Washington continued to make plans for Benedict Arnold.

Understandably, at this point, General Washington's main concern was to bring Arnold to justice. The Patriots were certain that Arnold still didn't realize that the Americans knew that he had become a traitor as he was left to command West Point as usual.

Benedict Arnold

Washington contacted a man who had been known as a gallant, intelligent, and loyal soldier to the Patriots, Sergeant John Champe, and beseeched him to undertake the dangerous task of capturing Arnold. Champe was a large man, full of bone and muscle, as well as courageous. He seemed the perfect soldier to undertake the capture of Arnold.

"Your mission will be, Sergeant Champe, to desert from General Lee's platoon and join the British in New York City as a traitor," announced General Washington. "You will imply to the Redcoats that you were inspired to defect because of the bravery of Benedict Arnold. With luck, you may gain Arnold's confidence and be put into Arnold's command."

"And what if I'm not put into his command?" asked Champe.

"You should still have the opportunity to watch Arnold closely. Having already admitted that Arnold's undaunted courage of defecting was your inspiration, Arnold should most possibly pay special attention to you."

Champe nodded.

Washington continued. "Try to study Arnold's routines and habits to reveal a plan of action to kidnap him. Assuming that the kidnapping will be successful, our men will then capture Arnold and take him back to New Jersey where I will be waiting." Washington paused for a moment to think. "I have one stipulation, John, and that is that you bring Arnold in alive."

"Yes, sir," responded Champe.

Champe was put into the platoon of General Henry Lee. After several weeks, Champe was called into Lee's office and ordered to desert that night. No help would be given to Champe, so he was to find his way to the British quarters as a real turncoat. At 11:00 p.m., Champe rode his horse out of camp.

About a half a mile out of camp, a mounted patrol challenged Champe. He kept quiet, pulled up his hood, and dug his spurs into his horse. The patrol belonged to Lee, who was awakened to learn of the incident. Lee played dumb and suggested that the man was a countryman in a hurry.

However, before long it was reported that John Champe was missing from his barracks, and a pursuit party was sent out to find him. By then, they assumed that the person in flight had been Champe. He was unable to ride toward New York at a gallop because of multiple checkpoints whose guards would set off a cry if they spotted a lone horseman running at full clip. It was past dawn when Champe finally arrived at New York's harbor.

Dismounting his horse and with a knapsack strapped on his

shoulders, Champe plunged into the water. A British officer observing the scene realized that an American defector was trying to reach them and ordered him to be taken aboard the ship.

Champe was questioned by British commander, Henry Clinton, who learned that Arnold's desertion had inspired Champe to also desert. Clinton found Champe's story believable, and he was placed into the force that Arnold commanded.

In the next few weeks, Champe planned to capture Arnold during one of their evening talks and render him unconscious. Finally, it was decided that a small boat would be sitting in the river on the evening of December 21 to take Arnold to General Washington. However, Champe and Arnold never arrived. It was later learned that Arnold's unit – in which Champe was serving – unexpectedly had shipped off to Virginia. Arnold was still at large, and the Culper Ring was still at risk because of the feasibility that Benedict Arnold might know of the Culpers' existence.

Months went by with no word from John Champe. Then one day, a bedraggled, bearded John Champe appeared in Lee's camp. After landing in the South, he had to pretend to be a Redcoat and fight the Patriots, Finally, he deserted – for real this time – from the British army and traveled only at night to evade discovery by the enemy.

Washington offered Champe a lavish award and a discharge from the military. However, Champe wanted to rejoin General Lee and his troop, but Washington feared that if Champe were ever taken prisoner, he would inevitably be recognized. Champe, therefore, took up Washington's offer and returned to his home in Virginia.

Benedict Arnold was never captured and left behind the legacy of being a traitor and a backhanded, cowardly character to his American country. He was never even a hero to the British and eventually died in England, a broken man.

Nathan heard of Arnold's treason and was anxious to relate the story to Elizabeth, who probably still thought of Arnold as a great American leader.

CHAPTER 14

LETTER FROM NATHAN AND
AT HOME IN LEXINGTON

Dearest Elizabeth,

My work continues not on the battlefields but near Washington's headquarters at Valley Forge. I was near the command post last week when John Andre was brought to be examined, condemned, and executed for treason. His crime had been delivering plans of West Point from Benedict Arnold. I saw him before execution, but I was on duty on that day and could not stay to see the actual lynching.

Andre was a Loyalist acting the part of a Patriot and helping Benedict Arnold. I thought of Nathan Hale who was executed as a spy. Hale had no trial and had no use of a Bible or clergyman in his last moments. Andre had every indulgence allowed to him.

Truly, though, we were all astonished when we heard that Benedict Arnold had become a turncoat. A loyal and trustworthy Patriot, he changed his allegiance and committed treason to America. It has been a grievous circumstance to witness that such a strong Patriot actually changed sides, and, we are told, that Arnold was disgruntled by too little pay and not enough attention to his work. So far, he has escaped and may have already returned to England.

General Washington is trying to end the standoff in New York so that he can head to the South. Washington has sent Nathanael Green ahead to fight the battles there until he himself is free. One of the greatest challenges will be to win the South.

I have a friend going to post this letter for me now. I pray for you and our family to remain in good health.

Your loving husband,

Nathan

* * * *

"We learned about the Battle at Cowpens today at school. It actually took place some time ago," said Nate, excitedly at supper time. "Want to know about it, Ma?"

"Well, yes. First a prayer for our food. Samuel will you say grace?"

"Lord, we thank you for this food as we know that many soldiers are going hungry. We wish that we could share this delicious supper. We thank you that Pa and all of the rest of our family are all believed to be safe. In Jesus name. Amen."

"Thank you, Samuel," said Elizabeth. Turning then to Nate, Elizabeth stated, "Well, tell me what you learned today, Nate."

"Well, first off, General Washington put Nathanael Greene in charge of the southern troops since Washington himself was not able to leave New York. Greene had only 1,500 men and was outnumbered three to one against Charles Cornwallis, so Greene split his men into two groups and asked Daniel Morgan to take half and march in another direction," summarized Nate.

"Wait," commented Hannah, "was Morgan's first name Daniel? I thought it was David."

"No, Nate's correct," chimed in Samuel. "It's Daniel. Go ahead, Nate."

"Cornwallis told Tarleton – don't remember his first name because it was a strange name – to attack Morgan. Morgan had his men form into three lines in a rolling meadow known as the Cowpens."

"That's a strange name, Cowpens," asserted Elizabeth.

Nate nodded.

"Well, the Americans completely annihilated the British, and it ended up being the second most decisive battle of the war so far," concluded Nate.

"What was the first?" asked Elizabeth.

"It was Trenton. Remember, Washington won it as well as Princeton, so he took the state of New Jersey?"

"Oh, yes, of course, I remember," replied Elizabeth.

"There's a bit more," added Patsy. "Cornwallis meanwhile had all of his men lighten their loads because they were going to follow Nathanael Greene. Cornwallis's men used all of their energy chasing Greene, but when they reached the Dan River, the Patriots were already on the other side. Cornwallis was upset that they had marched 200 miles just to see the Americans out of reach."

"But the story didn't really end well," inserted Samuel. "Ten days later, Greene and his 4,000 soldiers recrossed the Dan River and then followed Cornwallis. In March, they ended up at Guilford Courthouse, and Greene awaited an attack from Cornwallis. Unfortunately, Cornwallis won, and Greene was so upset that he left the army and returned home."

"I don't remember Pa writing in his letters about Cowpens," remarked Samuel.

"No, he hasn't, but you know how irregular and infrequent the letters are, so you have learned about it before Pa has written of the battle," responded Elizabeth. "I'm so proud of you children to know so much of the soon-to-be history of this war. I just want to hear that it's over and that your father is returning home."

* * * *

That night after supper was over and dishes were done, the family took a seat near the fire so that Elizabeth could read from the Bible. She had only gotten it open when there came a knock at the door.

"Children, go to the back room. Samuel, get the rifle and join me at the door."

"Who is it?" Samuel asked.

"Chaska," came the reply.

Elizabeth quickly opened the door to let Chaska in. With him pranced a beautiful tan and black dog, obviously Ranger.

"Children," summoned Elizabeth, as Samuel knelt down to grab Ranger by the neck in a huge hug. Samuel got his share of licks before the children crowded around Ranger.

`There was no keeping Beauty, Trusty, and Jewel away from Ranger, and everyone was laughing gleefully.

"It's so nice to see you, Little Bear. I'm sorry; I mean Chaska," said Elizabeth.

"It is all right to call me Little Bear. I know that Nathan would call me that, too. He is not back yet from the war?"

"No, but we got a letter today. Come into the kitchen and I'll read it to you."

The reunion with Little Bear and Ranger was the best thing that had happened to the family in quite a while, and the children simply couldn't get enough of Ranger.

"Little Bear, please stay for the night. Ma will make a place for you near the fire. We see very few people and seldom have any company. We are so happy to see both you and Ranger," commented Samuel, as he took a moment to introduce both Magdalena and Patsy to Little Bear.

"Where is Grace?" questioned Little Bear.

"She is helping in the army. She acts as a 'camp follower,'" answered Elizabeth.

"Oh, yes, I've heard such a term. Those women are essential in helping the soldiers," responded Little Bear.

The children had been watching silently as Little Bear signaled to Ranger a few times with his hands.

Finally, Nate asked, "Little Bear, does Ranger know sign language?"

"Yes, he does. I taught him a few easy signals, such as lay down, fetch the stick, and stand guard. He knows others, too, so he's quite clever, I think. They are, however, simple commands."

"That's great," responded Nate. "I knew Ranger was a smart dog. By the way, Little Bear, we still know the sign language for dog."

Everyone except Patsy and Magdalena signed "dog," and Little Bear displayed a wide smile.

"I want you to know, Little Bear, that everyone enjoyed either a coat or vest from the furs that you brought us last year," inserted Elizabeth.

"My vest was wonderful. My friends at school were jealous," Hannah declared with a broad grin.

"They really did make beautiful outerwear," stated Elizabeth. "Thank you."

Without his other two friends with him, Little Bear seemed to relax as he always did when he came to visit Nathan. He sat and told the children stories, drank tea, and enjoyed some freshly made bread.

"I have a story that I haven't told you before," commented Little Bear after he had told several stories that the children already knew.

"Do you know the name General Greene?" Little Bear asked.

Everyone nodded.

"It was one evening that General Greene needed to get a message to Colonel Sumter, and no one could be found to carry the word. One of our Oneida warriors is married to a white lady, and they both help out in Greene's platoon kind of like 'camp followers.' His name is Dakota and her name is Amala."

"What do their names mean?" asked Hannah.

"Dakota means 'friend,' and Amala means 'pure.' Well, anyway, General Greene finally asked Amala if she would deliver the message. She agreed."

"Why not ask Dakota?" questioned Nate.

"They thought it would look less conspicuous for a white female to be riding in the evening than a Native American male. He would likely be stopped and searched."

Everyone nodded in understanding.

"The general explained the message to Amala, but then he also wrote it down and gave her instructions to hide it in her moccasin. It was getting dusk when she was stopped by a British scouting party, and since she was coming from the direction of Greene's camp, they decided to detain her and search her. However, the men balked at performing the search of a young lady themselves and sent for a Loyalist matron.

"Amala took advantage of the delay, and she tore Greene's message into small pieces and ate them, piece by piece. When the matron arrived, the search revealed nothing, and Amala continued on to Colonel Sumter's camp."

"So Amala got stopped and searched anyway even though she was a white female," stated Samuel.

Little Bear nodded.

"That was a really good story," responded the Patsy.

"Tell us the story again about the roosters," stated Hannah when it seemed that Little Bear might have run out of tales.

"You love that story, don't you? I tell it nearly every time I come," said Little Bear, again smiling. "We went to a farmhouse one day several years ago. It was a big farmhouse outside of Boston. We really just wanted feathers from the lady's roosters, but we knew that she wouldn't give them to us if we asked."

"Why did you want the feathers?" questioned Patsy who hadn't heard the story before.

"For our head dress. We had jewelry with us and asked to trade it for some bread. She had no extra bread to give us, but we gave her the jewelry anyway and pretended to leave." Little Bear paused to ponder a moment.

"We waited outside behind the barn until we saw the roosters come out of the shed, and we grabbed them and pulled out their tail feathers. They squawked loudly, and the lady ran out to see if we were killing the roosters. She shook her fists at us, and we ran."

The children were hooting at the story. "I can just see this lady screaming and shaking her fists," said Patsy as she laughed. "However, you got your feathers."

Little Bear grinned and nodded.

Elizabeth made a place on the floor near the fire for Little Bear. All of the dogs gathered around Little Bear, and each found a spot for the night.

In the morning, Elizabeth made hot porridge for Little Bear and then packed a lunch for him and some bones for Ranger.

The children knew to get up early if they wanted to bid their two friends goodbye. They were up at dawn.

"Please come back again, Little Bear," pleaded Hannah. "We love it when you are here."

Little Bear nodded as the children gathered around to embrace him in a huge hug.

CHAPTER 15

SOUTHERN BATTLES
AND YORKTOWN

With the horrible camp conditions still gnawing at the Patriots, some started to mutiny with the hope of going home. It didn't look good for the Americans. By now, the Loyalists believed that the Southerners were pro-English, and only the Northerners were Rebels.

With the northern campaign becoming a stalemate, the British set their sights southward. It was, however, in the South that Loyalists to the King and Crown were being shot, tarred and feathered, and executed by the Patriots. Houses of the Loyalists to the king were being burned. It had become in reality a civil war: British plus southern Loyalists against the Patriots of the North.

Lafayette and Hoyt sat around the fire at Valley Forge one evening discussing the war.

"It's the fifth year of the war," stated Hoyt, "and our money is worthless here in America. In addition, I hear that the English economy is also in shambles. To be sure, economies on both continents are in a state of havoc."

"Yes, it's a terrible situation to be sure. Also, I heard that some of Washington's army have lost faith in being part of the

Top: "Washington Before Yorktown" by Rembrandt Peale

Bottom: Washington's hut at Yorktown

militia," continued Lafayette. "They have not been paid, and 1,500 of them filed out of camp on their way to Philadelphia."

"Yes, I heard the same," replied Hoyt. "In addition, Clinton in New York heard about the mutiny and caught up with fleeing soldiers. He tried to get them to renounce the American army totally and acquiesce to the British side, but the soldiers proclaimed that they were not defectors, only mutineers. Frankly, I wouldn't want to be either one. To me, they are both disgraceful."

"Apparently, once they got paid an extra ten dollars by the Philadelphia officials, they reenlisted." Lafayette paused. "In the beginning, everyone in the Continental Army was fighting for freedom. Now, unfortunately, some have turned to fighting for money."

Lafayette paused for a moment and then changed the subject. "I heard a term today that I haven't heard before. Trimmers. Do you know what it means?"

"Yes, I've heard the term, and I actually asked General Washington one day," responded Hoyt. "Washington said that the southern army troops are not well trained or organized and possess no loyalty. Thus, those soldiers called Trimmers have no real allegiance to either side. They drift from British army to Patriot army and vice versa. It's a very sad situation because an army troop can't really trust a Trimmer, who could change his allegiance at any time."

"How horrible. I don't know anyone in the North who could easily switch sides. Of course, there are spies, but they are not Trimmers. And then there are the Partisans in the South," commented Lafayette. "Do they also have no allegiance to one side or the other?"

"No, actually Partisans are rather mysterious men who are fighting differently than we Patriots," Hoyt said. "They are taking advantage of South Carolina's terrain to hide, strike, and kill. They don't fight in columns but rather use the brush, trees, and hills to cover themselves.

"I have to say that I originally learned to fight that way," continued Hoyt. "When I was growing up, my best friend was an Oneida Native American, and we used the environment for cover when hunting animals. At times, I think that it is still the best way to fight."

* * * *

General Washington and Hoyt sat one day in Washington's hut discussing how things were going in the North. Even with many disappointments on his plate, Washington tended to still be optimistic.

"For all of our difficulties, the United States has at least adopted a Constitution, and this spring, Congress has drafted, and the states have approved, the Articles of Confederation," asserted Washington. "I loved hearing the church bells and gun salute when the Articles were approved. It was a joyous event."

"It was indeed," maintained Hoyt.

"And a Pennsylvania newspaper reported, 'Thus, America is growing up into greatness even during the war.' That brought a smile to my face and joy to my heart," certified Washington.

Hoyt nodded and smiled. "The marquis and I were discussing how things were going in the South the other evening. What progress are we Patriots making?"

"There hasn't been much. As you know, we in the North have been locked in a standoff in New York," Washington admitted, "and I haven't had the opportunity to go to the South with troops. I have asked Nathanael Greene to take command of the southern forces. He has always been one of my favorite commanders, and I place total faith in his ability to commission the troops."

General Washington paused to think. "I have to say, though, that during this two-and-a-half-year deadlock with the British in New York, we still are waiting for the French-American alliance to bear fruit with a French navy. The French have delivered an army but no ships, and we really need the navy to harvest a real victory," concluded Washington.

It wasn't long after Washington's and Hoyt's discussion that General Jean-Baptiste de Rochambeau of France arranged thirty warships to sail from the West Indies to America's Chesapeake Bay to fight at Yorktown, Virginia, against General Charles Cornwallis. Some 13,000 troops were on the warships, led by Admiral Francois de Grasse.

In mid-summer, General Washington began to organize a large-scale movement of troops: 2,000 Patriots and nearly 5,000 French soldiers would march some 450 miles from New York to Yorktown, Virginia. In secrecy, they hid the strategy from Clinton, who was still in New York.

The plan worked because Clinton feared an attack on New York until the first part of September when he finally realized Washington had departed. Washington was anxious to know exactly where the French warships were during his march; however, the ships were already in Chesapeake Bay containing 13,000 French troops.

By now, Lafayette, Hamilton, and von Steuben, who were near Yorktown, learned that help was on the way. Washington and Rochambeau were heading south together while de Grasse was in Chesapeake Bay. Lafayette was given the huge task of keeping Cornwallis occupied in Virginia while the allies closed in from land and sea. Cornwallis would be essentially trapped.

Lafayette had a number of spies with him, and while he waited for Washington and Rochambeau, he decided to gain some intelligence. He sent one particular Black soldier – James Armistead – into Cornwallis's camp. Armistead gave Cornwallis false information about the Patriots while gathering intelligence about the British to take back to Lafayette. James Armistead's exploit helped to ensure that Cornwallis would be outmaneuvered.

In reality, the actual siege began on September 28 when nearly 9,000 American soldiers joined 8,000 French troops, and they surrounded Yorktown and Cornwallis's 6,000 soldiers. Adding in the navy troops in Chesapeake Bay, the swollen population of the Yorktown environs made it momentarily a rival of Philadelphia, the largest city in America at the time.

Trenches needed to be dug by the Patriots, and cannons put into place before the bombardment. Washington struck a few blows with a pickaxe so that it might be said that General Washington first broke ground.

On a clear, bright October morning – October 9 – Washington ceremoniously touched a match to a cannon and fired the first American gun. The newly adopted American flag was hoisted to announce the start of the Battle of Yorktown.

Not long after the start of the siege, General Cornwallis had to abandon his post for an underground bunker to pursue safety. On a dark, rainy night – October 14 – the French stormed one British redoubt (fortification) and the Americans, under the command of Lieutenant Colonel Alexander Hamilton, attacked another. Both redoubts fell. It was the biggest battle of the war.

General Washington retold the story of the defeat to the men who had remained in Valley Forge: "Cornwallis, who became desperate, prepared one last frantic attempt; he tried to cross Virginia by use of a river – as my troops had done on the Delaware – to escape to the north.

"However, on the night that he made his attempted maneuver, a wild storm blew in and scattered his small boats. Cornwallis was doomed, and he knew it."

The batteries began to halt their firing, and a British officer appeared carrying a white flag, accompanied by a drummer boy. Immaculate in their red coats and white trousers, two British soldiers walked slowly but proudly toward the allied lines.

A letter from a British soldier was presented to General Washington:

> *"Sir, I propose a cessation of hostilities for twenty-four hours, and that two officers be appointed by each side, to meet at Mr. Moore's house, to settle terms for the surrender of the posts at York and Gloucester."*

Ironically, Washington had no experience in such matters. In the eleven years and two wars in which Washington had been involved, no enemy army had ever formally surrendered to him.

However, as required, on the morning of October 19, 1781, King George's vanquished men marched out between rows of Americans and the French, leaving their swords in a neat pile. A British tune was played as the ceremony began; with a touch of irony, the British selected "The World Turned Upside Down."

General Charles Cornwallis did not attend; he pleaded illness and sent his sword with one of his soldiers, who rendered it into the hands of the Patriots.

Washington wrote a letter to Philadelphia: "I have the honor to inform Congress that the reduction of the British army under the command of General Cornwallis is most happily effective."

Marquis de Lafayette proclaimed the victory in a more abbreviated form: "The play is over."

Finally, Nathan had positive news to include in his letter to his beloved wife, Elizabeth

LETTER FROM NATHAN AND AT HOME IN LEXINGTON

Dearest Elizabeth,

With my new post, I was not present at the Battle of Cowpens in South Carolina, but the marquis told me about it, and I wanted you to know that we were successful in the battle. General Washington placed General Daniel Morgan in charge of our troops to fight Lieutenant Colonel Banastre Tarleton and his battalion. According to the marquis, Morgan decided to position his men in three successive lines. Being hit on three sides, Tarleton's line crumbled. We suffered only a few causalities, and the battle was a turning point in our conquest of South Carolina. So far, it was definitely a very decisive American victory in the war.

Our troops have fought our most current battle at Yorktown. My friend since the beginning of my time with General Washington has been Jonas Browning. He recounted the siege to me last night.

It was carried on for several days until most of the guns in the enemy's troops were silenced. Whenever our soldiers were to get ready to battle, the commander would yell "Rochambeau," who was the officer in charge of our French forces. It was a good watchword because when pronounced quickly, it sounded like "rush on boys." I found this to be a bit humorous. It was used often that day at Yorktown as the Patriots outdid the Redcoats.

The climax of the battle, I understand, was the capturing of two redoubts. One of the fortifications was taken by my friend, Alexander Hamilton, and the other was apprehended by the French. Once both of the redoubts were commandeered, the battle was essentially won. Cornwallis simply couldn't save the British. As the Redcoats silenced their guns, they played their drums and waved a white flag. The battle was over.

The next day, Jonas said, the British pleaded their release to just go home. Washington definitely wouldn't allow that since our Patriots were still being held captive in horrible conditions on the British ships after the battle of Charlestown.

Jonas recounted that about noon on the day after the battle ended, the American flag was hoisted to a ten-gun salute. He said that seeing the star-spangled banner waving majestically in the faces of our adversaries was a glorious sight.

On October 19, a ceremony was held for the end of the war, and we can only hope that it truly will end. If so, I will be coming home soon, and I pray that is true. I cannot fathom what you have gone through during these long, dreadful years of battle, and I can only continue my daily prayers that God has and continues to keep you safe.

I pray that I'll see all of you soon.

Your loving husband,

Nathan

* * * *

The nation watched as bedraggled men limped their way home. Thin and frail with ragged clothes and sometimes no shoes, these Patriots were the victors. Elizabeth fed everyone who stopped – whether Patriot or Loyalist.

The Loyalists and the Native Americans were the true losers of the war. The Loyalists lost their homes, livelihood, and land that they possessed in prewar America. Up to 80,000 Loyalists fled into exile, almost all with lives that were diminished.

Likewise, the Native Americans were left with nothing but heartache. When the British relinquished all the lands near the Mississippi River to the Patriots, they gave away the territories that the Native Americans had inhabited for centuries. In the fifty years that followed the Treaty of Paris of 1783, the United States of America would kill, subjugate, or banish all the Native Americans who lived in the territories won during the Revolutionary War.

Grace returned home before her father and was enthusiastically embraced by everyone in the family. The love and pride that each person felt for Gracie was unequivocal. She had grown into adulthood during the year that she had been gone, and it showed in everything that she did.

"For all of the heartache and toil that we all endured, I must say that I'm so glad that I did it," remarked Grace as she was caressed with hugs and showered with kisses. "I saw things that I'll never talk about, at least not for many years, and I truly wonder what atrocities Pa saw."

"We may never know," said Elizabeth. "I'm betting that he'll never talk about them."

Grace nodded in agreement.

"I was near to Washington's camp last winter," she continued, "and I heard that Marquis de Lafayette was there. Since Pa was friends with both Washington and Lafayette, I was hopeful that perhaps he was there. As it turned out, he had been there but wasn't any longer. I never saw Pa, but I feel sure he's alive and on his way home."

"We all pray for that moment when he rides up the path," Elizabeth professed.

It was but several weeks later that Nathan arrived with his two best friends – Jonas Browning and Thomas Franklin – who were headed to the northwestern part of Massachusetts.

The Hoyt family members were ecstatic. They had all tried to imagine the moment when Nathan would arrive home, but the happiness that they had imagined was nowhere near the euphoria that they actually experienced. Nathan couldn't stop kissing his children and wife as he twirled each of them into the air and embraced them in huge bear hugs. The children shrieked and cried out at the reunion, and Elizabeth, who wasn't prone to weeping, let the tears roll freely down her cheeks.

Beds were quickly prepared in the spare bedroom, and several trips were made to the cellar to collect extra food for the welcoming feast. It was a gala event – one that everyone had originally anticipated for the Christmas of 1775. In the end, it would be ninety-eight blood-drenched months later with the signing of the 1783 Treaty of Paris.

The children did most of the cooking so that their ma and pa could sit together. In reality, Nathan insisted that Elizabeth sit right next to him so that he could hold her hand. Periodically, he would kiss her on the cheek, his face beaming. Never having seen their parents act this way, the children found it winsome and enduring as they snuck glances. Exuberance showed in their eyes as they, too, were overwhelmed at seeing their pa.

The conversation that night centered around anything but the battles. Elizabeth tried to keep the conversation light and focused on happy events.

The three men found many stories to share with the family about incidents that had happened during the five years without mention of fighting and bloodshed. One of the favorite stories that was told was about a lady named Patsy. Of course, Patsy McDonald Hoyt loved the tale the most.

"This story happened back in the early part of the war," stated Nathan. "It was at the home of Patsy and John Calder. Their homestead was near Philadelphia and General Washington. I was with the general at the time, so I had access to hearing the story. Anyway, it was close to General Howe's Redcoat encampment as well, and he decided to put up some of his commanders in a fine house for the winter. He chose Calder's home.

"Well, the Calders were given a room for themselves upstairs, and the rest of the house was inhabited by the British. One night, Howe was having a meeting, and he ordered the Calders to retire early. Patsy thought that it was obvious that something important was on the agenda.

"As the British started their meeting, Patsy snuck down the stairs and put her ear to the keyhole. Listening intently, she heard that the British were planning an attack on Washington on December 4. Now, it was one thing to get the information, and it was another to relay it to Washington.

"Finally, she decided to request a pass to go to a nearby village for flour, and the British officer at the gate of Patsy's town allowed it. Patsy trudged through the snow to General Washington's encampment and personally delivered the message of the impending attack. When the British made their move on the American army, we were ready, armed, and waiting."

"What an incredible story, Pa," Samuel stated.

"There were many times when we were assisted by American colonists who risked their lives for us," commented Thomas. "We owe so much to those loyal colonists who brought us messages, fed us, or offered us a place to stay for the night."

"Indeed, that is so true," chimed in Jonas. "I'll tell just a short story about Martha, who posed as a spy for us in General Clinton's encampment. Soldiers believed that women who were helping in the camps knew nothing about military equipment. However, Martha's husband had repaired cannons, guns, and other weapons used by the army, so she knew a great deal. Martha's reports back to Washington on cannons and munitions were thorough and extremely useful."

"I also posed as a spy for a short time," said Gracie in a soft voice.

Everyone was silent, thinking that they had misunderstood her.

"What did you say, Gracie?" asked Elizabeth.

"Yes, you heard me correctly. I posed as a spy for a while. I was stationed in a British encampment, and after the men decided that I was trustworthy, I was privy to most of their secret conversations. I would slip out at night and get the messages to General Washington. I…I…I'm sorry, but I can't talk anymore about it. I just knew that I was doing my best for my country."

Grace received hugs from everyone as Elizabeth wiped her eyes, knowing that her daughter had risked her life for her country. Little did she know that Nathan had done the same.

After this, the conversation seemed to hit a lull as everyone looked tired and ready to call it a night. However, Samuel wanted to make an announcement before everyone dispersed to bed. "Before we all leave, Magdalena and I have some news to share."

Samuel nudged Magdalena, who was beaming as she spoke.

"I'm expecting a new little Hoyt."

The atmosphere became jubilant. Pats on the back and congratulations were given to the young Hoyt couple. Nathan put his arm around his wife, and they sat beaming at the good news.

"This new little Hoyt will be brought into a free country – the United States of America," declared Nathan.

Because they had no wine, Elizabeth arose to put a pot of water on the fire to heat. Knowing that this exuberant news had to have a toast, they would celebrate with what they did have – tea!

Soon, Nathan's two friends rose to say goodnight, and Nathan clasped each of their hands.

"You both have been symbols of virtue, courage, and endurance to me. God put us together for a purpose," Nathan continued, "and General Washington was given leadership for a definite reason. Not only did he hold his army together, but he also supported a war-weary nation until the decisive victory was won."

Not only these three men, but also all surviving soldiers knew that they would never again savor the camaraderie they had felt with fellow soldiers, the overwhelming, pulsating tremor of danger, or the exhilaration of a battle victory that had come from serving the infant nation in its quest for independence.

"Washington Resigning His Commission" by John Trumbell

CHAPTER 17

AFTER YORKTOWN

The war continued, though, for two more years. Yorktown was the Patriots' last real battle with the British. King George, however, reacted with stubborn optimism, thinking that once the British had recovered, they would resume the war with America. It never happened.

On March 28, 1782, word reached New York City that the British House of Commons voted to end all offensive strikes in America; however, that by no means signified the end of militia activity.

On April 12, 1782, the British navy fought two battles against the French on opposite sides of the planet – in the crystal Caribbean near Guadeloupe and in the waters around India. It wasn't until eight years, two months, and nine days after Lexington that the war ceased. On September 3, 1783, the treaty of peace between the world's greatest empire and a nation of farmers was signed in Paris.

November 25, 1783, was named Evacuation Day of New York City. It was the capstone of the Revolutionary War. The military, officers, and colonists had suffered so long during the war, and it was on this day that the British were finally leaving New York City. The sky gave way to fireworks and people rejoiced. The city went wild.

It was on this day, too, that in a local pub, George Washington said goodbye to his officers. All who attended the dinner knew that the function was less for dining and more for saying farewell. It soon became an emotional meeting.

Washington had no speech to read, and he could hardly trust his voice for the few words he spoke: "With a heart full of love and gratitude, I now take leave of you. I most devoutly wish that your later days may be as prosperous and happy as your former ones have been glorious and honorable. I shall feel obliged if each of you will come and take me by the hand."

Instead of taking Washington's hand, each officer threw his arms around the shoulders of this bulky, courageous friend. Many were weeping, and, through it all, no one spoke a word. For many it had been eight years of serving General Washington. Through Valley Forge and Morristown, through Brandywine and Monmouth, through mutiny, starvations, and near defeat – all of it had been worth it to serve the general, who by now was a hero.

Thus, Washington and his Continental Army had won the war for independence because the general had defeated the British by outlasting them, by staying alive, by keeping the troops moving, by relying on intelligence from his Culper Spy Ring, and by not giving in. It had been a war of attrition.

No one man was trusted as much as Washington had been. He was America's hero. The general resigned and was ready to resume civilian life in Mount Vernon, with no intention of ever recommencing the role of a public figure. He arrived in Mount Vernon on Christmas Eve, 1783.

After he left the military, Washington often visited the frontier – the place that made America different from Europe. Before the war, it was this area that had been banned by the British, and colonists were not supposed to venture. Unfortunately, the Europeans were trapped; their countries were full of people and the land was totally inhabited. If the colonial frontier were open, then America would become much more inviting, and Europe would lose valuable citizens.

However, after the war, Washington made many escapades to the frontier land, sleeping under the stars or staying with people who lived in log cabins – people who never expected to be visited by the most famous person in the world.

When the time came to elect the first President of the United States, George Washington didn't want the position. It wasn't a capstone that he envisioned in his career. However, on April 1, 1789, the American hero was sworn in as the first President of the United States of America.

During his eight years as President, Washington shaped the very institutions that made America what it has become because his vision of the country continued to grow.

Washington's legacy remains yet today; Americans take pride in citizenship, sacrifice, honor, and integrity. More than any other man, Washington made the American experiment – as he called it – a success.

* * * *

It is believed that none of the Culpers ever divulged what they had done during the war. Almost as if the war had never happened, they resumed their normal lives.

Major Benjamin Tallmadge – born in 1754 – was among those officers who were present on November 25, 1783, when Washington bid his comrades adieu in the New York City tavern before returning to Mount Vernon. Tallmadge made a visit to Long Island – from which Patriots had been banished for seven years – to be reunited with his family and friends. After marrying the daughter of a wealthy Long Island landowner, Tallmadge settled as a merchant and banker as well as a postmaster in Litchfield, Connecticut. He would later serve sixteen years in the House of Representatives. Tallmadge died in 1835.

Following the war, Captain Caleb Brewster – who was born in 1747 and died in 1827 – got married and raised a large family. He farmed and assumed a job with the U.S. Revenue-Marines. That particular job had been established by Congress for armed enforcement of custom laws of the new nation.

Abraham Woodhull – born in 1750 and died in 1826 – remained in Setauket, marrying a cousin and raising three children. He served as Suffolk County Magistrate and held other positions of authority in the county government.

Sergeant John Champe was born in 1752 and died 1798. He was married and had six children. In 1939, there was a monument erected on the farm in Virginia where he had lived. A placard there read, "Here was the house of Sergeant John Champe of the Continental Army. Champe pretended desertion and joined the British in an attempt to capture Benedict Arnold. Failing, he rejoined the American Army." General Washington placed the greatest confidence in Champe.

Anna Strong was born in 1740 and died in 1812. She lived out the rest of her life with her Patriot husband, Selah Strong, who had spent part of his incarceration on a British prison ship.

James Rivington was born in 1724 and briefly published a newspaper without the word "Royal" in the title but was shut down by Patriots, whom he had antagonized with his earlier loyalty to the British. He spent the rest of his life in poverty and died in 1802.

Austin Roe was born in 1748, achieving the rank of captain while in the army. Roe operated a tavern in East Setauket, where George Washington overnighted on a tour of Long Island in

1790. There is no evidence that Washington ever knew that Roe was part of the Culper Ring. Roe married and raised a family of eight. He died in 1830.

Agent 355 (who was not in reality Anna Strong) whose name and fate have both been lost in time, may have escaped imprisonment on a British ship during the war and gone on to live a happy life. Or she may have passed away on one of the dark, dreadful, and infested British ships held in New York harbor during the war. For convenience sake, I made Anna Strong 355 in this book, but, in reality, the woman titled 355 is not known by name. She did, however, exist in the Culper Ring.

Nathan Hoyt (who was not in reality a part of the Culper Ring) was born in 1719. After the war, he returned to his home, which was actually Norwalk, Connecticut, near New York City. Nathan lived out his life as a farmer with all eleven children nearby. Elizabeth passed away and he married Sarah, with whom he lived out the rest of his life. He passed away in 1799.

IN CONGRESS, JULY 4, 1776.

A DECLARATION

BY THE REPRESENTATIVES OF THE

UNITED STATES OF AMERICA,

IN GENERAL CONGRESS ASSEMBLED.

Signed by ORDER and in BEHALF of the CONGRESS,

JOHN HANCOCK, PRESIDENT.

ATTEST.
CHARLES THOMSON, SECRETARY.

PHILADELPHIA: PRINTED BY JOHN DUNLAP.

ABOUT THE AUTHOR

JAN FRAZIER has been in the field of education for over forty years – first in secondary schools and most recently at the university level. Having retired in the spring of 2020 from Bradley University, she planned to spend much of her time traveling. However, the pandemic hit, and she fell into teaching 7-8 grade English at Good Shepherd Lutheran School. Once a teacher, always a teacher!! Jan hopes that there are traveling days ahead. She has taken students to Europe for many years and believes that only so much can be taught within the four walls of the classroom, and then not only students but also teachers need to get into the world to "see" for themselves. Jan has been honored with various awards for teaching as well as for her writing abilities. She has twenty-three books to her credit.

"The Birth of Old Glory" by Percy Moran

Works Cited

The American Revolution. Documentary. 2015.

Auricchio, Laura. *The Marquis Lafayette Reconsidered.* Penguin Random House. New York: 2014.

Berkin, Carol. *Revolutionary Mothers.* Random House. New York: 2005.

Cobbs, Elizaabeth. *The Hamilton Affair.* Arcade Publishing. New York: 2016.

Edwards, Franklin. *Diary of Agent 355.* Pilar Publishing. California: 2017.

Ferling, John. *Almost a Miracle.* Oxford University Press. New York: 2007.

The First American. Video. 2016.

Hoyt, David Webster. *A Genealogical History of the Hoyt Haight, and Hight Families.* Providence Press Co. Boston: 1871.

Kilmeade, Brian. *George Washington's Secret Six.* Penguin Random House. New York City: 2016.

Martin, Joseph. *A Narrative of a Revolutionary Soldier.* Penguin Books. New York: 2001.

McCullough, David. *1776.* Simon and Schuster Paperbacks. New York City: 2005.

McDowell, Bart. *The Revolutionary War.* National Geographic Society. Washington, D.C.: 1983.

The Patriot. Video. 2000.

River, Charles. *The Culper Ring.* Charles River Editors: 2018

Rose, Alexander. *Washington's Spies.* Random House. New York, New York: 2007.

Silent Night. Hallmark Entertainment. 2002.

Simmons, Michael. *Alexander Hamilton: First Architect of the American Government.* Make Profits Easy LLC. New York: 2016.

TURN: Washington's Spies. Season 1. 2014.

TURN: Washington's Spies. Season 2. 2015

TURN: Washington's Spies. Season 3. 2016

TURN: Washington's Spies. Season 4. 2017

War for a New Nation. Video. 2001.

www.hellgatepress.com

www.ingramcontent.com/pod-product-compliance
Lightning Source LLC
Chambersburg PA
CBHW051518170626
46811CB00002B/890